A Pair Of Schoolgirls
A Story Of School Days

by

Angela Brazil

Double 9
BOOKS

A Pair Of Schoolgirls
A Story Of School Days
by Angela Brazil

ISBN: 978-93-61421-30-3

Published by

DOUBLE 9 BOOKS

2/13-B, Ansari Road
Daryaganj, New Delhi – 110002
info@double9books.com
www.double9books.com
Tel. 011-40042856

ABOUT THE AUTHOR

Angela Brazil was born on November 30, 1868, and died on March 13, 1947. She was one of the first British writers of "modern schoolgirls' stories," which were written from the point of view of the characters and were meant more for entertainment than to teach morals. Brazil first started writing when she was 10 years old. She and her close childhood friend Leila Langdale made a magazine based on the children's magazine Little Folks, which Brazil loved at the time. There were riddles, short stories, and poems in the "publications" of the two girls. In their magazines, both girls wrote serials. Brazil's was called "Prince Azib." Brazil wrote Little Folks later in life. She didn't start writing until later in life when she became very interested in Welsh mythology. Angela Brazil is thought to be the first author of girls' school stories who wrote from the student's point of view and whose stories were mostly meant to entertain rather than teach moral lessons.

CONTENTS

CHAPTER I
A SCHOOL ELECTION

It was precisely five minutes past eleven on the first day of the autumn term, and Avondale College, which for seven whole weeks had been lonely and deserted, and given over to the tender mercies of paperhangers, painters, and charwomen, once more presented its wonted aspect of life and bustle. The reopening was a very important event in the opinion of everybody concerned, partly because it marked the beginning of a fresh school year, and partly because the building had been altered and enlarged, many changes made in the curriculum, and many new names added to the already long list in the register. Three hundred and eighty-seven pupils had assembled that morning in the great lecture hall, the largest number on record at the College; five additional classes had been formed, and there were six extra mistresses. At the eleven o'clock interval the place seemed swarming with girls; they thronged the staircase and passages, filled the pantry, blocked the dressing-rooms, and overflowed into the playground and the gymnasium — girls of all sorts and descriptions, from the ten-year-olds who had just come up (rather solemn and overawed) from the Preparatory to those elect and superior damsels of seventeen who were studying for their Matriculation.

By the empty stove in the Juniors' Common Room stood half a dozen "betwixt-and betweens", whose average age probably worked out at fourteen and a quarter, though Mavie Morris was a giantess compared with little Ruth Harmon. The six heads were bent together in closest proximity, and the six tongues were particularly active, for after the long summer holidays there was such a vast amount to talk about that it seemed almost impossible to discuss all the interesting items of news with sufficient rapidity.

"The old Coll. looks no end," said Grace Russell. "It's so smart and spanky now—one hardly knows it! Pictures in the classrooms, flowers on the chimneypieces, a stained glass window in the lecture hall, busts on brackets all along the corridor wall, and the studio floor polished! Every single place has been done up from top to bottom."

"I'd like it better if it didn't smell so abominably of new paint," objected Noëlle Kennedy. "When I opened the studio door, the varnish stuck to my fingers. However, the school certainly looks much nicer. Why, even the book cupboard has been repapered."

"That's because you splashed ink on the wall last term. Don't you remember how fearfully cross Miss Hardy was about it?"

"Rather! She insisted that I'd done it on purpose, and couldn't and wouldn't believe it was an accident. Well, thank goodness we've done with her! I'm glad teachers don't move up with their forms. I'm of the opposite opinion to Hamlet, and I'd rather face the evils that I don't know than those I do. Miss Pitman can't possibly be any worse, and she may chance to be better."

"I say, it's rather a joke our being in the Upper Fourth now, isn't it?" remarked Ruth Harmon.

"I'm glad we've all gone up together," said Dorothy Greenfield. "There's only Marjory Poulton left behind, and she won't be missed. We're exactly the same old set, with the addition of a few new girls."

"Do you realize," said Mavie Morris, "that we're the top class in the Lower School now, and that one of us will be chosen Warden? There'll be an election this afternoon."

"Why, so there will! What a frantic excitement! We shall all have to canvass in the dinner-hour. I wonder if Miss Tempest has put up the list of candidates yet? I vote we go to the notice board and see; there's just time before the bell rings."

Off scrambled the girls at once, pushing and jostling one another in their eagerness to get to the lecture hall. There was a crowd collected round the notice board, but they elbowed their way to the front notwithstanding. Yes, the list was there, in the head mistress's own handwriting, and they scanned it with varying comments of joy or disappointment, according as their names were present or absent.

"Hurrah!"

"Disgusting!"

"No luck for me!"

"I don't call it fair!"

"You're on, Dorothy Greenfield, and so am I."

"I say, girls, which of you'll promise to vote for me?"

Avondale College was a large day school. Its pupils were drawn from all parts of Coleminster and the surrounding district, many coming in by train or tramcar, and some on bicycles. Under the headmistress-ship of Miss Tempest its numbers had increased so rapidly that extra accommodation had become necessary; and not only had the lecture hall and dressing-rooms been enlarged, but an entire new wing had been added to the building. Avondale prided itself greatly upon its institutions. It is not always easy for a day school to have the same corporate life as a boarding school; but Miss Tempest, in spite of this difficulty, had managed to inaugurate a spirit of union among her pupils, and to make them work together for the general good of the community. She wished the College to be, not merely a place where textbooks were studied, but a central point of light on every possible subject. She encouraged the girls to have many interests outside the ordinary round of lessons, and by the help of various self-governing societies to learn to be good citizens, and to play an intelligent and active part in the progress of the world. A Nature Study Union, a Guild of Arts and Crafts, a Debating Club, a Dramatic Circle, and a School Magazine all flourished at Avondale. The direction of these societies was in the hands of a select committee chosen from the Fifth and Sixth Forms, but in order that the younger girls might be represented, a member of the Upper Fourth was elected each year as "Warden of the Lower School", and was privileged to attend some of the meetings, and to speak on behalf of the interests of the juniors.

Naturally this post was an exceedingly coveted honour: the girl who held it became the delegate and mouthpiece of the lower forms, an acknowledged authority, and the general leader of the rest. It was the custom to elect the warden by ballot on the afternoon of the reopening day. Six candidates were selected by Miss Tempest, and these were voted for by the members of the several divisions of the Third and Fourth Forms.

Among the six chosen for this election, none was more excited about her possible chances than Dorothy Greenfield, and as our story centres round her and her doings she merits a few words of description. She was a tall, slim, rather out-of-the-common-looking girl, and though at present she was passing through the ugly duckling stage, she had several good points, which might develop into beauty later on. Her large dark grey eyes, with their straight, well-marked brows, made you forgive her nondescript nose. She lacked colour, certainly, but her complexion was clear, and, despite her rather thin cheeks, the outline of her face was decidedly pleasing. Her mouth was neat and firm, and her chin square; and she had a quantity of wavy, fluffy brown hair that had an obstreperous way of escaping from its ribbon and hanging over her ears. During the past six months Dorothy had shot up like Jack's beanstalk, and she was still growing fast—an awkward process, which involved a certain angularity of both body and mind. She was apt to do things by fits and starts; she formed hot attachments or took violent prejudices; she was amiable or irritable according to her mood, and though capable of making herself most attractive, could flash out with a sharp retort if anybody offended her. She had a favourable report in the school: she was generally among those marked "excellent" in her form, and she was above the average at hockey and tennis, had played a piano solo at the annual concert, won "highly commended" at the Arts and Crafts Exhibition, and contributed an article to the School Magazine.

Possessing such a good all-round record, therefore, Dorothy might have as reasonable a possibility of success as anybody else at the coming election, and she could not help letting her hopes run high. The ballot was to be taken at half-past three, which left little time for canvassing; but she meant to do the best for herself that circumstances would allow. She was a day boarder, so, when morning classes were over, she strolled into the Juniors' Common Room to discuss her chances. Already some papers were pinned up claiming attention for the various candidates:

"Vote for Val Barnett, the hockey champion."

"Hope Lawson begs all her friends to support her in the coming election."

"Grace Russell solicits the favour of your votes."

"Noëlle Kennedy relies upon the kindness of the Lower School."

"Hallo, Dorothy!" said Mavie Morris. "Aren't you going to add your quota to the general lot? All the others are getting up their appeals. I wish Miss Tempest had put me on the list of likelies!"

"I can't think why she didn't," replied Dorothy. "I should say you're far more suitable than Noëlle Kennedy."

"Why, so do I, naturally. But there! it can't be helped. I'm not among the elect, so I must just grin and bear it. Is this your appeal? Let me look."

She seized the piece of paper from Dorothy's hand, and, scanning it eagerly, read the following lines:

> Ye voters at the school election,
> I beg you'll look in my direction;
> I hate to boast and brag, but yet
> For once I'm blowing my own trumpet.
> Now don't you think in me you'd find
> A candidate suited to your mind?

No bookworm I, but fond of sports,
Hockey or games of other sorts;
At acting I can run the show,
And play my part, as well you know.
At meetings all your wants I'd state,
And make a speech at the debate.
I'd back in all scholastic storms
The interests of the Lower Forms.
A zealous leader I should be,
So when you vote, please remember me!
I hope these verses you will pardon,
And choose me for the Lower School Warden.

"What do you think of it?" asked Dorothy. "I made it up during the history lesson, and wrote it on my knee under the desk. One wants something rather different from other people's, and I thought perhaps no one else would have a rhyming address."

"It's not bad," commented Mavie, "but you do brag."

"I've apologized for it. One must state one's qualifications, or what's the use of being a candidate? Look at Val's notice—she calls herself the hockey champion."

"No one takes Val too seriously. I don't believe she's the ghost of a chance, though she did win the cup last season. One needs more than that for a warden; brains count as well as muscles."

"I know; that's why I tried poetry."

"Please don't call that stuff poetry. Half of the lines won't scan."

There was a pucker between Dorothy's dark eyebrows as she snatched back her literary bantling.

"I don't suppose that matters. Everybody isn't so viper-critical," she retorted. "Shall I pin it up here or in the gym.?"

"It will be more seen here; but I warn you, Dorothy, I don't think the girls will like it."

"Why not?"

"Well, it's clever enough, but it's cheeky. I'm afraid somehow it won't catch on. If you take my advice, you'll tear it up and just write 'Vote for Dorothy Greenfield' instead."

But taking other people's advice was not at present included in Dorothy's scheme of existence; she much preferred her own ideas, however crude.

"I'll leave it as it is," she answered loftily. "It can't fail to attract attention anyhow."

"As you like. By the by, if you're going round canvassing, there's been a new — —"

But Dorothy did not wait to listen. She was annoyed at Mavie's scant appreciation of her poetic effort; and having manifested her independence by pinning the offending verses on the notice board, she stalked away, trying to look nonchalant. She was determined to use every means at hand to ensure success, and her best plan seemed to be to go round personally soliciting votes.

"I'll tackle the dinner girls now," she thought, "and I expect there'll be just time to catch the others when they come back in the afternoon. Thank goodness the election is only among the Third and Fourth! It would be terrible if one had to go all round the school. Why, I never asked Mavie! How stupid! But she's certain to be on my side; she detests Val, and she's not particularly fond of Hope either, though of course there's Grace. Had I better go back and make sure of her?"

On the whole she decided that as she had left Mavie in rather a high and mighty manner, it would seem a little beneath her dignity to return at once and beg a favour, so she went into the playground instead to beat up possible electors. She was not the first in the field, by any means. Already Valentine Barnett and her satellites were hard at work coaxing and wheedling, while the emissaries of Doris Earnshaw and Noëlle Kennedy were urging the qualifications of their particular favourites. Hope Lawson was seated on the see-saw in company with a number of small girls from the Lower Second.

"What's she doing that for?" thought Dorothy. "Those kids haven't got votes. It's sheer waste of time to bother with them. She's actually put her arm round that odious little Maggie Muir, and taken Nell Boughton on her knee! I shouldn't care to make myself so cheap. I suppose she's letting Blanche Hall and Irene Jackson do her canvassing for her."

Dorothy was, however, too much occupied with her own affairs to concern herself greatly about her neighbours' movements. To put her claims adequately before each separate elector was no mean task, and time fled all too quickly. She used what powers of persuasion she possessed, and flattered herself that she had made an impression in some quarters; but very few of the girls would give any definite promises. Many of them, especially those of the Middle and Lower Thirds, seemed to enjoy the importance of owning something which it was in their power to withhold.

"I'm waiting till I've heard what you all six have to say for yourselves," said Kitty Palgrave condescendingly. "I shan't make up my mind until the very last minute."

"It's so difficult to choose between you," added Ellie Simpson, a pert little person of twelve.

Their tone verged on the offensive, and in any other circumstances Dorothy would have administered a snub. As it was, she pocketed her pride, and merely said she hoped they would remember her. She heard them snigger as she turned away, and longed to go back and shake them; but discretion prevailed.

"One has to put up with this sort of thing if one wants to get returned Warden," she reflected. "All the same, it's sickening to be obliged to truckle to young idiots like that."

She had not by any means found all the possible voters, so she decided to return to the Juniors' Common Room. Mavie had gone, but a number of other girls stood near the notice board talking, and reading the appeals of the various candidates. Dorothy strolled up to see how her verses were being received. They made a different impression on different minds, to judge from the comments that met her ears.

"It's ripping!" exclaimed Bertha Warren.

"Says she can run the show, does she?" sneered Joyce Hickson.

"I call it just lovely!" gushed Addie Parker.

"Her trumpeter's dead, certainly!" giggled Phyllis Fowler. "Hallo, Dorothy! I didn't see you were there."

"I'm going to vote for you, Dorothy," said Bertha, "and so is Addie. Phyllis has promised Hope, and Joyce is on Val's side. If you like, I'll canvass for you here, while you do the gym. You'd better not waste any time, because the others are hard at it, and it's best to get first innings if you can."

Dorothy hastily agreed, and hurried off to the gymnasium, where she was fortunate enough to catch some of her own classmates. They were all sucking enormous peppermint "humbugs", and were almost speechless in consequence; but they had the politeness to listen to her, which was more than she had experienced from some of the girls.

"Very sorry!" replied Annie Gray, talking with difficulty. "You should have asked us sooner. Val's been round, and simply coerced us."

"She made it a hockey versus lacrosse contest, and of course we plumped for hockey," murmured Elsie Bellamy.

"Val's simply ripping at hockey!"

"Is that all you care for?" exclaimed Dorothy scornfully. "Val has nothing else to recommend her."

"Hasn't she? What about peppermint 'humbugs'? I call them a very substantial recommendation."

"Did Val give you those?"

"Rather! She put on her hat and bolted out into High Street and bought a whole pound. Lucky Miss James didn't catch her as she dodged back!"

"She's handing them round to everybody," added Helen Walker. "I wish I had taken two."

For once Dorothy's pale cheeks put on a colour. She could not restrain her indignation.

"How atrociously and abominably mean!" she burst out. "Why, it's just bribery, pure and simple. I didn't think Val was capable of such a sneaking trick. She knows quite well how unfair it is to the rest of us."

"Why, you could have done the same if you'd liked," laughed Elsie. "It's not too late now. I've a preference for caramels, if you ask me."

"I'd be ashamed!" declared Dorothy. "Surely you ought to give your votes on better grounds than 'humbugs' or caramels? Such a thing has never been done before at the Coll."

"All the more loss for us," giggled Helen flippantly.

"Do you mean to tell me you don't care whether a candidate behaves dishonourably or not?"

"Not I, if she's jolly."

"I'm disgusted with you, absolutely disgusted! If you haven't a higher ideal of what's required in a warden, you don't deserve to have votes at all."

"Draw it mild, Dorothy!" chirped Elsie.

"I won't. I'll tell you what I think of you: you're a set of greedy things! There isn't one of you with a spark of public spirit, and if the election is going to be run on these lines, I— —"

But Dorothy's tirade was interrupted by the dinner bell; and the objects of her scorn, hastily swallowing the offending peppermints, decamped at a run, leaving her to address a group of empty chairs. She followed more leisurely, fuming as she went. She knew she had been foolish and most undiplomatic to lose her temper so utterly, but the words had rushed out before she could stop them.

"They wouldn't have voted for me in any case," she said to herself, "so it really doesn't matter, after all, they're only a minority. I expect it will prove a very even affair, perhaps a draw, and that no one will have a complete walk-over."

CHAPTER II
WHAT DOROTHY OVERHEARD

At half-past three, exactly in the middle of the French reading-lesson, Miss James, the school secretary, entered the Upper Fourth room with a sheaf of voting papers in her hand. These were dealt round to all the girls, with the exception of the candidates, and Miss James gave a brief explanation of what was required.

"On each paper you will find six names. You must put a cross to the one you wish to choose for your warden. Do not write anything at all, but fold the paper and hand it in to Miss Pitman, who will place it in this box, which I shall call for in five minutes."

So saying, she bustled away in a great hurry to perform a similar errand in the next classroom. The six candidates tried to sit looking disinterested and unconscious while their fates were being decided. Hope Lawson hunted out words in the dictionary, Valentine Barnett made a parade of arranging the contents of her pencil box, and the others opened books and began preparation. Not a word was allowed to be spoken. In dead silence the girls recorded their crosses and handed in their papers, and the last was hardly dropped into the ballot box before Miss James reappeared. The result of the election was to be announced at four o'clock, therefore there were still twenty minutes of suspense. Miss Pitman went on with the French reading as if nothing had happened, and Dorothy made a gallant effort to fix her attention on *Le Jeune Patriote*, and to forget that Miss Tempest and Miss James were hard at work in the library counting votes. Nobody's translation was particularly brilliant that afternoon; everyone was watching the clock and longing for the end of the lesson. When the bell rang there was a general scuffle; books were seized and desk lids banged, and though Miss Pitman called the Form to order and insisted upon a decorous exit from the room, the girls simply pelted down the stairs to the lecture hall. In a few moments the whole school had assembled. There was not long to wait, for exactly at the stroke of four Miss Tempest walked on to the platform and made the brief announcement:

"Hope Lawson has been elected Warden of the Lower School by a majority of fifty votes."

Dorothy left the lecture hall with her head in a whirl. That Hope should have won by such an enormous majority was most astonishing. She could not understand it. Conversation was strictly forbidden on the staircase, but the moment she reached the gymnasium door she burst into eager enquiries.

"Yes, it's a surprise to everybody," said Ruth Harmon. "I thought myself that Val would get it. All the Lower Fourth and most of the Upper Third were for her."

"Then how could Hope possibly score by fifty?"

"She did it with the kids, I suppose."

"But the First and Second weren't voting?"

"Indeed they were! Do you mean to say you never knew? Why, Miss James gave it out this morning."

"Of all sells!" gasped Dorothy. "I heard nothing about it! It's the first year those kids have ever taken part in the election. Why couldn't some of you tell me?"

"I was just going to," said Mavie, "but you stalked away and wouldn't listen. It's your own fault, Dorothy."

"You might have run after me."

"You looked so lofty, I didn't feel disposed."

"Val didn't know either," interposed Bertha Warren. "She never canvassed in the First or the Second; no more did Grace or Noëlle. I'm not certain if any of you knew except Hope. Only a few were in the room when Miss James gave it out."

"Then she's taken a most mean advantage," said Dorothy. "I understand now why she was sitting on the see-saw making herself so extremely pleasant. It's not fair! Miss James ought to have announced to the whole school that such a change had been made."

"Go and tell her so!" sneered Phyllis Fowler.

"Those who lose always call things unfair," added Joyce Hickson.

Dorothy walked away without another word. She did not wish to be considered jealous, and her common sense told her that she had already said more than enough. She was too proud to ask for sympathy, and felt that her most dignified course was to accept her defeat in silence. She thought she would rather not speak even to her friends, so, ignoring violent signals from Bertha Warren and Addie Parker, she went at once to put on her outdoor clothes. The dressing-room, to provide greater accommodation, had not only hooks round the walls, but double rows of hat-stands down the middle, with lockers for boots underneath. As Dorothy sat changing her shoes, she could hear three girls talking on the other side of the hat-stand, though, owing to the number of coats which were hanging up, the speakers were hidden from her. She recognized their voices, however, perfectly well.

"I'm rather surprised at Hope getting it," Helen Walker was saying. "I thought Val was pretty safe. I voted for her, of course."

"A good many voted for Dorothy," replied Evie Fenwick.

"I know. I thought she might have had a chance even against Val. She'll be dreadfully disgusted."

"I'm very glad Hope was chosen," said Agnes Lowe. "After all, she's far the most suitable for Warden; she's ever so much cleverer than Val."

"But not more than Dorothy!"

"No; but she's a girl of better position, and that counts for something. Her father was Mayor last year, and her mother is quite an authority on education, and speaks at meetings."

"Well, Dorothy's aunt writes articles for magazines. One often sees the name 'Barbara Sherbourne' in the newspapers. Dorothy's tremendously proud of her."

"Dorothy needn't take any credit to herself on that account," returned Agnes, "for, as it happens, Miss Sherbourne isn't her aunt at all; she's no relation."

"Are you sure?"

"Absolutely. I know for a fact that Dorothy is nothing but a waif, a nobody, who is being brought up for charity. Miss Sherbourne adopted her when she was a baby."

At this most astounding piece of information, Dorothy, who had followed the conversation without any thought of eavesdropping, flung her slippers into her locker and stalked round to the other side of the hat-stand.

"Agnes Lowe, what do you mean by telling such an absolute story?" she asked grimly.

"I'd no idea you were there!" returned Agnes.

"Listeners never hear any good of themselves," laughed Helen.

"I'm extremely glad I overheard. It gives me a chance to deny such rubbish. I shall expect Agnes to make an instant apology."

Dorothy's tone was aggressive; she waited with a glare in her eyes and a determined look about her mouth. Agnes did not flinch, however.

"I'm sorry you heard what I said, Dorothy," she replied. "It wasn't meant for you; but it's true, all the same, and I can't take back my words."

"How can it be true?"

Agnes put on her hat hastily and seized her satchel.

"You'd better ask Miss Sherbourne. Probably everyone in Hurford knows about it except yourself. Come, Helen, I'm ready now," and she hurried away with her two friends, evidently anxious to escape further questioning.

Dorothy took up her pile of home-lesson books and followed them; but they must have raced down the passage, for when she reached the door they were already disappearing round the corner of the playground. It was useless to think of pursuing them; she had barely time, as it was, to catch her train, and she must walk fast if she meant to be at the station by half-past four. She scurried along High Street, keeping a watchful eye on the town hall clock in the intervals of dodging passengers on the pavements and dashing recklessly over crossings. At Station Road she quickened her footsteps to a run, and tore up the flight of stairs that was the shortest cut to the ticket office. Fortunately she possessed a contract, so she had no further delay, and was able to scuttle across the platform into the Hurford train. The guard, who knew her well by sight, smiled as he slammed the door of her compartment.

"A near shave to-day, missy! I see you're back at school," he remarked, then waved his green flag.

Dorothy sank down breathlessly. To miss the 4.30 would have meant waiting three-quarters of an hour—a tiresome experience which she had gone through before, and had no desire to repeat. She was lucky, certainly; but now that the anxiety of catching the train was over, the reaction came, and she felt both tired and cross. What an enormously long time it seemed since she had started that morning, and what a horrid day it had been! She leaned back in a corner of the compartment and took a mental review of everything that had happened at school: her expectation of winning the election, her canvassing among the girls, their many ill-natured remarks, Val's method of bribery, and Hope's unfair advantage. She was bitterly chagrined at missing the wardenship, and the thought that she might have had a chance of success if she had known of the voting powers of the First and Second Forms only added to her disappointment. She was indignant and out of temper with Mavie, with Hope, with the whole of her little world; everything had seemed to go wrong, and, to crown all, Agnes Lowe had dared to call her a nobody and a charity child! What could Agnes mean? It was surely a ridiculously false accusation, made from spite or sheer love of teasing. She, Dorothy Greenfield, a waif! The idea was impossible. Why, she had always prided herself upon her good birth! The Sherbournes were of knightly race, and their doings were mentioned in the county history of Devonshire as far back as Queen Elizabeth's reign. Of course, her name was Greenfield, not Sherbourne; but she was of the same lineage, and she had pasted the family crest inside her school books. She would trace out her pedigree that very evening right to Sir Thomas Sherbourne, who helped to fit out a ship to fight the Armada; and she would take a copy to school to-morrow and show it to Agnes, who could not fail to be convinced by such positive evidence. Yes, the girls should see that, far from being a nobody, she was really of a better family than Hope Lawson, whose claims to position rested solely on her father's public services to the city of Coleminster.

And yet under all her assurance there lurked an uneasy sensation of doubt. She had taken it for granted that her mother was a Sherbourne; but she remembered now that when she had spoken of her as such, Aunt Barbara had always evaded the subject. Nobody ever mentioned her parents. She had thought it was because they were dead; but surely that was not a sufficient reason for the omission? Could there be another and a stronger motive for thus withholding all knowledge about them? Several things occurred to her—hints that had been dropped by Martha, the maid, which, though not comprehended, had remained in her memory—looks, glances, half-spoken sentences let fall by Aunt Barbara's friends—a hundred nothings too small in themselves to be noticed, but, counted in the aggregate, quite sufficient to strengthen the unwelcome suspicion that had suddenly awakened.

"Rubbish!" thought Dorothy, with an effort to dispel the black shadow. "I'll ask Aunt Barbara, and I've no doubt she'll easily explain it all and set everything right."

By this time the train had passed Ash Hill, Burnlea, and Latchworth, and had arrived at Hurford, Dorothy's station. She stepped out of the compartment, so preoccupied with her reflections that she would have forgotten her books, if a fellow-passenger had not handed them to her. She scarcely noticed the Rector and his children, who were standing on the platform, and, turning a deaf ear to the youngest boy, who called to her to wait for them, she hurried off alone along the road.

It was a pleasant walk to her home, between green hedges, and with a view of woods and distant hills. Hurford was quite a country place, and could boast of thatched cottages, a market cross, and a pair of stocks, although it lay barely twelve miles from the great manufacturing city of Coleminster. Dorothy's destination was a little, quaint, old-fashioned stone house that stood close by the roadside at the beginning of the village street. A thick, well-clipped holly hedge protected from prying eyes a garden where summer flowers were still blooming profusely, a strip of lawn was laid out for croquet, and a small orchard, at the back, held a moderate crop of pears and apples. Dorothy ran in through the creeper-covered porch, slammed her books on the hall table, then, descending two steps, entered the low-ceiled, oak-panelled dining-room, and rushed to fling her arms round a lady who was sitting doing fancy work near the open window.

"Here I am at last, Auntie! Oh, I feel as if I hadn't seen you for a hundred years! I'm in the Upper Fourth, but it's been a hateful day. I never thought school was so horrid before. I'm very disappointed and disgusted and abominably cross."

"Poor little woman! What's the matter?" said Aunt Barbara, taking Dorothy's face in her hands, as the girl knelt by her side, and trying to kiss away the frown that rested there. "You certainly don't look as if you had been enjoying yourself."

"Enjoying myself? I should think not! We had an election for the wardenship, and my name was on the list, and I might perhaps have won if the others hadn't been so mean; but I didn't, and Hope Lawson has got it!"

"We can't always win, can we? Never mind! It's something that your name was on the list of candidates. All the girls who lost will be feeling equally disappointed. Suppose you just forget about it, go and take off your things, and tell Martha to make some buttered toast."

Dorothy laughed. Already her face had lost its injured and woeful expression.

"That's as good as saying: 'Don't make a fuss about nothing'. All right, Auntie, I'm going. But I warn you that this is only a respite, and I mean to give you a full and detailed list of all my particular grievances after tea. So make up your mind to it, and brace your dear nerves!"

Miss Barbara Sherbourne was a most charming personality. She was young enough to be still very pretty and attractive, but old enough to take broad views of life, and to have attained that independence of action which is the prerogative of middle age. She was a clever and essentially a cultured woman; she had lived abroad in her youth, and the glamour of old Italian cities and soft, southern skies still seemed to cling to her. She was a good amateur musician, could sketch a little, and had lately obtained some success in writing. Ever since Dorothy could remember, she and Aunt Barbara and Martha, the maid, had lived together at Holly Cottage, a particularly harmonious trio, liking their own mode of life, and quite independent of the outside world. The little house seemed to fit its inmates, and, in spite of its small accommodation, to provide just what was wanted for each. First there was the old-fashioned dining-room, with its carved oak furniture, blue china, and rows of shining pewter; its choice prints on the walls, its bookshelves, overflowing with interesting volumes; and the desk where Aunt Barbara wrote in the mornings—a room that seemed made especially for comfort, and reached its acme of cosiness on a cold winter's day, when arm-chairs were drawn up to the blazing fire that burnt in the quaint dog grate. Then there was the little drawing-room, with its piano and music rack, and its great Japanese cabinet, full of all kinds of treasures from foreign places. When Dorothy was a tiny girl it had been her Sunday afternoon treat to be allowed to investigate the mysteries of this cabinet, to open its numerous drawers and sliding panels, and to turn over the miscellaneous collection of things it contained; and she still regarded it in the light of an old friend. The artistic decorations, the chintz hangings, the water-colour paintings of Italian scenes, all helped to give an æsthetic effect to the room, and to make a very pleasant whole. The kitchen was, of course, Martha's particular domain, but even here there were books and pictures, and a table reserved for writing desk and work basket. I fear Martha did not often busy herself with pens and paper, for she held head-learning in good-natured contempt; but she appreciated her mistress's effort to make her comfortable, and polished the brass-topped inkpot diligently, if she seldom used it. Peterkin, the grey Persian cat, generally sat in the arm-chair, or on Martha's knee, which he much preferred, when he got the chance; and Draco, the green parrot, hobbled up and down his perch at the sunny window, repeating his stock of phrases, begging for titbits, or imitating smacking kisses.

Just at the top of the stairs was Dorothy's special sanctum. It had formerly been her nursery, and still contained her old dolls' house, put away in a corner, though her toys were now replaced by schoolgirl possessions. Here she kept her tennis racket, her hockey stick, her camera and photographic materials, her collections of stamps, crests, and picture postcards; there was a table where she could use paste or glue, or indulge in various sticky performances forbidden in the dining-room, and a cupboard where oddments could be stored without the painful necessity of continually keeping them tidily arranged. She could try experiments in sweet making, clay modelling, bookbinding, or any of the other arts and crafts that were represented at the annual school exhibition; in fact, it was a dear, delightful "den", where she could conduct operations without being obliged to move her things away, and might make a mess in defiance of Martha's chidings.

Dorothy often took a peep into her sanctum on her return from Avondale, but to-day she ran straight to her bedroom. She was anxious to finish tea and have a talk with Aunt Barbara. She felt she could not rest until she had mentioned Agnes Lowe's remarks, and either proved or disproved their truth. It was not a question that she could raise, however, when Martha was coming into and going out of the dining-room with hot water and toast; and it was only after she had cajoled Miss Sherbourne to the privacy of the summer-house, and had related her other school woes, that the girl ventured to broach the subject.

"I know it's nonsense, Auntie, but I thought I'd like to tell you, all the same," she concluded, and waited for a denial with a look of anxiety in her eyes that belied her words.

Miss Sherbourne did not at once reply. Apparently she was considering what answer to make.

"I knew you would ask me this some day, Dorothy," she said at last. "It seemed unnecessary for you to know before, but you are growing older so fast that it is time you learnt your own story."

Dorothy turned her face sharply away. She did not want even Aunt Barbara to see how her mouth was quivering.

"Is it true, then?" she asked, in a strangled voice.

"Yes, dear child. In a sense it is all absolutely true."

CHAPTER III
A RETROSPECT

More than thirteen years before this story begins, Miss Barbara Sherbourne happened to be travelling on the Northern Express from Middleford to Glasebury. She had chosen a corner of the compartment with her back to the engine, had provided herself with books and papers, had ordered a cup of afternoon tea to be brought from the restaurant car precisely at four o'clock, and had put a piece of knitting in her handbag with which to occupy herself in case she grew tired of reading or watching the landscape. After these preparations she anticipated a comfortable journey, and she leaned back in her corner feeling at peace with herself and all the world. Her fellow-passengers consisted of two old ladies, evidently returning home after a holiday in the South; a morose-looking man with a bundle of Socialist tracts, and a middle-aged woman, who, with a baby on her knee, occupied the opposite corner. Nobody spoke a word, except an occasional necessary one about the opening or closing of a window, and all settled down to read books and papers, or to enjoy the luxury of a snooze while the train sped swiftly northwards. The baby was sleeping peacefully, its lips parted, its long lashes resting on its flushed cheeks, and one little hand flung out from under the white woolly shawl which was wrapped closely round it. It made a pretty picture as it lay thus, and Miss Sherbourne's eyes returned again and again to dwell on the soft lines of the chubby neck and dimpled chin. She was fond of studying her fellow-creatures, and she could not quite reconcile the appearance of the child with that of the woman who held it in her arms. The latter was plainly though tidily dressed, and did not look like an educated person. There was nothing of refinement in her face: the features were heavy, the mouth even a trifle coarse. Her gloveless hands were work-worn, and her wedding ring was of a cheap gold. The general impression she gave was that of a superior working woman, or the wife of a small tradesman. The baby did not resemble her in the least: it was fair, and pretty, and daintily kept, its bonnet and coat and the shawl in which it was wrapped were of finest quality, and the tiny boot that lay on the carriage seat was a silk one.

Miss Barbara could not help speculating about the pair. She amused herself first with vainly trying to trace a likeness, then with wondering whether the woman were really the mother of the child, and if so, how she managed to dress it so well, and whether she realized that its clothes looked out of keeping with her own attire. Finally she gave up guessing, in sheer despair of arriving at any possible conclusion.

The train had been ten minutes late in starting, and was making up for lost time by an increase in speed as it dashed across a tract of moorland. The oscillation was most marked, and walls and telegraph posts seemed to fly past so quickly as to dazzle the sight. Miss Sherbourne closed her eyes; the whirling landscape made her head ache, and the swaying of the carriage had become very unpleasant. She took hold of the strap to steady herself, and was debating whether it would be better to close the rattling window, when, without further warning, there came a sudden and awful crash, the impact of which hurled the baby on to her knee, and telescoped the walls of the compartment. For a few seconds she was stunned with the shock. When she recovered consciousness she found herself lying on her side under a pile of wreckage, instinctively clutching the little child in her arms. She moved her limbs cautiously, and satisfied herself that she was unhurt; part of the roof had fallen slantwise, and by so doing had just saved her from injury, penning her in a corner of the overturned carriage. The smashed window was underneath, about eighteen inches above the ground, for the train in toppling over had struck a wall, and lay at an inclined angle.

From all around came piteous groans and cries for help, but Miss Sherbourne could see nobody, the broken woodwork cutting her off completely from the rest of the compartment. The baby in her arms was screaming with fright. Fortunately for herself, she preserved presence of mind and a resourceful brain. She did not lose her head in this emergency, and her first idea was to find some means of escape. She stretched out her hand and broke away the pieces of shivered glass till the window beneath her was free; then, still clasping the child, she managed to crawl through the opening on to the line below. So narrow was the space between the ground and the wreckage above her that she was forced to lie flat and writhe herself along. It was a slow and painful progress, and the light was so dim that she could scarcely see, while at any moment she expected to find her way blocked by fallen woodwork. Yet that was her one chance of safety, and at any cost she must persevere. She never knew how far she crawled; to her it seemed miles, though probably it was no greater distance than the length of the carriage: but at last she spied daylight, and, struggling through a hole above her head, she climbed over the ruins of a luggage compartment, and so on to the bank of grass edging the line.

The wind was blowing strongly over the moor, so strongly that she had difficulty in keeping her feet as she staggered into the shelter of the wall. The scene before her was one of horror and desolation. She saw at once the cause of the accident—the express had dashed into an advancing train, and the two engines lay smashed by the terrific force of the collision. A few passengers who, like herself, had managed to make their escape stood by the line—some half-dazed and staring helplessly, others already attempting to rescue those who were pinned under the wreckage. The guard, his face livid and streaming with blood, was running to the nearest signal box to notify the disaster, and some labourers were hurrying from a group of cottages near, bringing an axe and a piece of rope. To the end of her life Miss Barbara will never recall without a shudder the pathetic sights she witnessed as the injured were dragged from the splintered carriages. But the worst was yet to come. Almost immediately a cry of "Fire!" was raised, and the flames, starting from one of the overturned engines and fanned by the furious wind, gained a fierce hold on the broken woodwork, which flared up and burned like tinder.

"Come awa'!" screamed a countrywoman, seizing Miss Sherbourne almost roughly by the arm. "You with a bairn! Bring it to our hoose yonder out o' the wind. The men are doing a' they can, and we canna help 'em. It's no fit sight for women. Come, I tell ye! Th' train's naught but a blazin' bonfire, and them as is under it's as good as gone. Don't look! Don't look! Come, in the Lord's name!"

"Then may He have mercy on their souls!" said Miss Barbara, as with bowed head she allowed herself to be led away.

The news of the accident was telegraphed down the line, and as speedily as possible a special train, bearing doctors and nurses, arrived on the spot. The sufferers were carried to the little village of Greenfield, close by, and attended to at once, some who were well enough to travel going on by a relief train, while others who were more seriously injured remained until they could communicate with their friends. The fire, meanwhile, had done its fatal work, and little was left of any of the carriages but heaps of charred ashes. Those who had escaped comparatively unhurt had, with the aid of the few farm labourers who were near at the time, worked with frantic and almost superhuman endeavour to rescue any fellow-passengers within their reach; but they had at last been driven back by the fury of the flames and forced to abandon their heroic task. No one could even guess the extent of the death roll. From the extreme rapidity with which the fire had taken hold and spread, it was feared that many must have perished under the wreckage, but their names could not be ascertained until the news of the disaster was spread over the country, and their friends reported them as missing.

Twenty-four hours later Miss Barbara Sherbourne sat in the parlour of the Red Lion Hotel at Greenfield. She had remained there partly because she was suffering greatly from shock, and partly because she felt responsible for the welfare of the little child whom she had been able to save. The account of its rescue was circulated in all the morning papers, so she expected that before long some relation would arrive to claim it. The woman who had accompanied it was not among the list of the rescued, and Miss Barbara shuddered afresh at the remembrance of the burning carriages.

"It's a bonnie bairn, too, and takes wonderful notice," said Martha, Miss Sherbourne's faithful maid, for whom she had telegraphed. "Those to whom it belongs will be crazy with joy to find it safe. Dear, dear! To think its poor mother has gone, and to such an awful death!"

The baby girl was indeed the heroine of the hour. The story of her wonderful escape appealed to everybody; newspaper reporters took snapshots of her, and many people begged to be allowed to see her out of sheer curiosity or interest. So far, though she had been interviewed almost continuously from early morning, not one among the numbers who visited her recognized her in the least. Fortunately she was of a friendly disposition, and though she had had one or two good cries, she seemed fairly content to be nursed by strangers, and took readily to the bottle that was procured for her. At about six o'clock Miss Barbara and Martha sat alone with her in the inn parlour. The afternoon train had departed, bearing with it most of yesterday's sufferers and their friends, so it was hardly to be expected that any more visitors would arrive that evening. The baby sat on Miss Barbara's knee, industriously exercising the only two wee teeth it possessed upon an ivory needlecase supplied from Martha's pocket. Outside the light was fading, and rain was beginning to fall, so the bright fire in the grate was the more attractive.

"I'm glad we didn't attempt to go home to-night, Martha," said Miss Sherbourne. "I expect I shall feel better to-morrow, and I shall leave much more comfortably when this little one has been claimed. No doubt somebody will turn up for her in the morning. It's too late for anyone else to come to-day."

"There's a carriage arriving now," replied Martha, rising and going to the window. "Somebody's getting out of it. Yes, and she's coming in here, too, I verily believe."

Martha was not mistaken. A moment afterwards the door was opened, and the landlord obsequiously ushered in a stranger. The lady was young, and handsomely dressed in deep mourning. Her face was fair and pretty, though it showed signs of the strongest agitation. She was deadly pale, her eyes had a strained expression, and her lips twitched nervously. Without a word of introduction or explanation she walked straight to the child, and stood gazing at it with an intensity which it was painful to behold, catching her breath as if speech failed her.

"Do you recognize her?" asked Miss Barbara anxiously, turning her nursling so that the light from the lamp fell full on its chubby face.

"No! No!" gasped the stranger. "I don't know it. I can't tell whose it is in the least."

She averted her face as she spoke; her mouth was quivering, and her hands trembled.

"You've lost a baby of this age in the accident, maybe?" enquired Martha.

"No; I have lost nobody. I only thought—I expected——" She spoke wildly, almost hysterically, casting swift, uneasy glances at the child, and as quickly turning away her eyes.

"You expected?" said Miss Sherbourne interrogatively, for the stranger had broken off in the middle of the sentence.

"Nothing—nothing at all! I'm sorry to have troubled you. I must go at once, for my carriage is waiting."

"Then you don't know the child?"

"I don't," the stranger repeated emphatically; "not in the slightest. I tell you I have never seen it in my life before!"

She left the room as abruptly as she had entered, without even the civility of a good-bye; addressed a few hurried words in a low tone to the landlord in the hall, then, entering her conveyance, drove off into the rapidly gathering darkness.

"There's something queer about her," said Martha, watching the departure over the top of the short window blind. "She was ready to take her oath that she'd never set eyes on the child before, but the sight of it sent her crazy. Deny what she may, if you ask me, it's my firm opinion she was telling a lie."

"Surely no one would refuse to acknowledge it!" exclaimed Miss Barbara. "She seemed so terribly agitated and upset, she must have expected to find some other baby, and have been disappointed."

"Disappointed!" sniffed Martha scornfully. "Aye, she was disappointed at finding what she expected. Agitated and upset, no doubt, but the trouble was, she knew the poor bairn only too well."

In spite of the publicity given by the newspapers, no friends turned up to claim the little girl. Nobody seemed to recognize her, or was able to supply the least clue to her parentage. It was impossible even to ascertain at what station the woman, presumably her mother, had joined the train. She was already settled in the corner when Miss Sherbourne entered the compartment, and though a description of her was circulated, none of the porters remembered noticing her particularly. All the carriages had been full, and there had been several other women with young children in the accident. Any luggage containing papers or articles which might have led to her identification had been destroyed in the fire. The baby's clothing was unmarked. Day after day passed, and though many visits were paid and enquiries made, the result was invariably the same, and in a short time popular interest, always fleeting and fickle, died completely away.

After staying nearly a fortnight at the Red Lion Hotel, in the hope that the missing relatives might come at last to the scene of the disaster, Miss Sherbourne returned to her own home, taking with her the child which so strange a chance had given into her charge. For some months she still made an endeavour to establish its identity; she put advertisements in the newspapers and enlisted the services of the police, but all with no avail: and when a year had passed she realized that her efforts seemed useless. Her friends urged her strongly to send the little foundling to an orphanage, but by that time both she and Martha had grown so fond of it that they could not bear the thought of a parting.

"I'll adopt her as my niece, if you're willing to take your share of the trouble, Martha," said Miss Barbara.

"Don't call it trouble," returned Martha. "The bairn's the very sunshine of the house, and it would break my heart if she went."

"Very well; in future, she's mine. I shall name her Dorothy Greenfield, because Dorothy means 'a gift of God', and it was at Greenfield that the accident occurred. I feel that Fate flung her into my arms that day, and surely meant me to keep her. She was a direct 'gift', so I accept the responsibility as a solemn charge."

Miss Sherbourne's decision met with considerable opposition from her relations.

"You're quixotic and foolish, Barbara, to think of attempting such a thing," urged her aunt. "It's absurd, at your age, to saddle yourself with a child to bring up. Why, you may wish to get married!"

"No, no," said Miss Barbara hastily, her thoughts on an old heartache that obstinately refused to accept decent burial; "that will never be—now. You must not take that contingency into consideration at all."

"You may think differently in a year or two, and it would be cruelty to the child to bring her up as a lady and then hand her over to an institution."

"I should not do her that injustice. I take her now, and promise to keep her always."

"But with your small means you really cannot afford it."

"I am sure I shall be able to manage, and the child herself is sufficient compensation for anything I must sacrifice; she's a companion already."

"Well, I don't approve of it," said Aunt Lydia, with disfavour. "If you want companionship, you can always have one of your nieces to stay a week or two with you."

"It's not the same; they have their own homes and their own parents, and are never anything but visitors at my house. However fond they may be of me, I feel I am only a very secondary consideration in their lives. I can't be content with such crumbs of affection. Little Dorothy seems entirely mine, because she has nobody else in the world to love her."

"Then you actually intend to assume the full responsibility of her maintenance, and to educate her in your own station—a child sprung from who knows where?"

"Certainly. I shall regard her absolutely as my niece, and I shall never part with her unless someone should come and show a higher right than mine to claim her."

Having exhausted all their arguments, Miss Sherbourne's relatives gave her up in despair. She was old enough to assert her own will and manage her own affairs, and if she liked to spend a large proportion of her scanty income on bringing up a foundling,—well, she need not expect any help from them in the matter. They ignored the child, and never asked it to their houses, refusing to recognize that it had any claim to be treated on an equality with their own children, and disapproving from first to last of the whole proceeding.

It was part of Miss Barbara's plan to let little Dorothy grow up in complete ignorance of her strange history. She did not wish her to realize that she was different from other children, or to allow any slight to be cast upon her, or any unkind references made to her dependent position. For this reason she removed into Yorkshire, and settled down at the village of Hurford, where the circumstances of the case were not known, and Dorothy could be received as her niece without question. She left the little girl at home with Martha when she went to stay with her relations, whom she succeeded in influencing so far that she persuaded them to refrain from all allusions to Dorothy's parentage when they paid return visits to Holly Cottage. Dorothy had often wondered why Aunt Lydia and Aunt Constance treated her so stiffly, but, like most children, she divided the world into nice and nasty people, and simply included them in the latter category, without an inkling of the real reason for their coldness. That she was never asked to their homes did not trouble her in the least; she would have regarded such a visit as a penance. Martha kept the secret rigidly. In her blunt, uncompromising fashion she adored the child, and was glad to have her in the house. Though she did not spare scoldings, and enforced a rigorous discipline concerning the kitchen regions, she looked after Dorothy's welfare most faithfully, especially during Miss Sherbourne's absence, and always took the credit for having a half-share in her upbringing.

And now more than thirteen years had passed away, and the chubby baby had grown into a tall girl who must be verging upon fourteen. Time, which had brought a line or two to Miss Barbara's face, and a chance grey thread among her brown locks, had also brought her a modest measure of success. She had always possessed a taste for literary work, and in the quiet village of Hurford she had been able to write undisturbed. Her articles, reviews, and short stories appeared in various magazines and papers, and by this method of adding to her income she had been able to send Dorothy to Avondale College. It was quite an easy journey by train from Hurford to Coleminster, and the school was considered one of the best in the north of England. The girl had been there for four years, and had made satisfactory progress, though she had not shown a decided bent for any special subject. What her future career might be, Fate had yet to determine.

CHAPTER IV
DOROTHY MAKES A FRIEND

Dorothy set off for school on the morning after the election in a very sober frame of mind. Aunt Barbara had made her acquainted with most of the facts mentioned in our last chapter, and she now thoroughly understood her own position. To a girl of her proud temperament the news had indeed come as a great humiliation. Instead of bringing a copy of her pedigree to convince Agnes Lowe that she was one of the Sherbournes of Devonshire, she would now be obliged to ignore the subject. She did not expect it would be mentioned openly again, but there might be hints or allusions, and the mere fact that the girls at school should know was sufficiently mortifying.

"Agnes was perfectly right," she thought bitterly. "I am a waif, a nobody, with no relations, and no place of my own in the world. I suppose I am exactly what she called me—a charity child! I wonder how she heard the story? But it really does not matter who told her; the secret has leaked out somehow, and no doubt it will soon be bruited all over the College. It was time I knew about it myself; but oh dear, how different I feel since yesterday!"

Thus Dorothy mused, all unconscious that the shuttle of Fate was already busy casting fresh threads into the web of her life, and that the next few minutes would bring her a meeting with one whose fortunes were closely interwoven with her own, and whose future friendship would lead to strange and most unexpected issues. The train had reached Latchworth, where a number of passengers were waiting on the platform. The door of Dorothy's compartment was flung open, and a girl of about her own age entered, wearing the well-known Avondale ribbon and badge on her straw hat. Dorothy remembered noticing her among the new members who had been placed yesterday in the Upper Fourth, though she had had no opportunity of speaking to her, and had not even learnt her name. A pretty, fair-haired lady was seeing her off, and turned to Dorothy with an air of relief.

"You are going to the College?" she asked pleasantly. "Oh, I am so glad! Then Alison will have somebody to travel with. Will you be good-natured, and look after her a little at school? She knows nobody yet."

"I'll do my best," murmured Dorothy.

THE NEW GIRL

"It will be a real kindness. It is rather an ordeal to be a complete stranger among so many new schoolfellows. Birdie, you must be sure to come back with this girl, then I shall feel quite happy about you. You have your books and your umbrella? Well, good-bye, darling, until five o'clock."

The girl stood waving her hand through the window until the train was out of the station, then she came and sat down in the seat next to Dorothy. She had a plump, rosy, smiling face, very blue eyes, and straight, fair hair. Her expression was decidedly friendly.

Dorothy was hardly in a genial frame of mind, but she felt bound to enter into conversation.

"You're in the Upper Fourth, aren't you?" she began, by way of breaking the ice.

"Yes, and so are you. Aren't you Dorothy Greenfield, who was put up for the Lower School election?"

"And lost it!" exclaimed Dorothy ruefully. "I don't believe I'll ever canvass again, whatever office is vacant. The thing wasn't managed fairly. You haven't told me your name yet."

"Alison Clarke, though I'm called Birdie at home."

"Do you live at Latchworth?"

"Yes, at Lindenlea."

"That pretty house on the hill? I always notice it from the train. Then you must have just come. It has been to let for two years."

"We removed a month ago. We used to live at Leamstead."

"How do you like the Coll.?"

"I can't tell yet. I expect I shall like it better when I know the girls. I'm glad you go in by this train, because it's much jollier to have somebody to travel backwards and forwards with. Mother took me yesterday and brought me home, but of course she can't do that every day."

Dorothy marched into school that morning feeling rather self-conscious. She could not be sure whether her story had been circulated or not, but she did not wish it to be referred to, nor did she want to enter into any explanations. She imagined that her classmates looked at her in rather a pitying manner. The bare idea put her on the defensive. Her pride could not endure pity, even for losing the Wardenship, so she kept aloof and spoke to nobody. It was easy enough to do this, since Hope Lawson was the heroine of the hour, and the girls, finding Dorothy rather cross and unsociable, left her to her own devices. At the mid-morning interval she took a solitary walk round the playground, and at one o'clock, instead of joining the rest of the day boarders in the gymnasium, she lingered behind in the classroom.

"What's wrong with Dorothy Greenfield?" asked Ruth Harmon. "She's so grumpy, one can't get a word out of her."

"Sulking because she missed the election, I suppose," said Val Barnett.

"That's not like Dorothy. She flares up and gets into tantrums, but she doesn't sulk."

"And she doesn't generally bear a grudge about things," added Grace Russell.

"I believe I can guess," said Mavie Morris. "I heard yesterday that she isn't really Miss Sherbourne's niece at all; she was adopted when she was a baby, and she doesn't even know who her parents were."

"Well, she can't help that."

"Of course she can't; but you know Dorothy! She's as proud as Lucifer, and Agnes Lowe called her a waif and a nobody."

"Agnes Lowe wants shaking."

"Well, she didn't mean Dorothy to overhear her. She's very sorry about it."

"I'm more sorry for Dorothy. So that's the reason she's looking so glum! Isn't she coming to the meeting?"

"I don't know. She's up in the classroom."

"Someone fetch her."

"I'll go," said Mavie. "It's a shame to let her stay out of everything. She's as prickly as a hedgehog to-day, and will probably snap my head off, but I don't mind. She may have a temper, but she's one of the jolliest girls in the Form, all the same."

"So she is. It's fearfully hard on her if what Agnes Lowe says is really true. I vote we try to be nice to her, to make up."

"Any girl who refers to it would be a cad."

"Well, look here! Let us try to get her made secretary of our 'Dramatic'."

"Right you are! I'll propose her myself."

Mavie ran quickly upstairs to the classroom.

"Aren't you coming, Dorothy? It's the committee meeting of the 'Dramatic', you know. The others are all waiting; they sent me to fetch you."

"You'll get on just as well without me," growled Dorothy, with her head inside her desk.

"Nonsense! Don't be such a goose. I tell you, everybody's waiting."

"Dorothy's jealous of Hope," piped Annie Gray, who, as monitress, was performing her duty of cleaning the blackboard.

"I'm not! How can you say such a thing? I don't care in the least about the Wardenship."

"Then come and show up at the meeting, just to let them see you're not sulking, at any rate," whispered Mavie. "Do be quick! I can't wait any longer."

Dorothy slammed her desk lid, but complied. Though she would rather have preferred her own society that day, she did not wish her conduct to be misconstrued into jealousy or sulks.

"Go on, Mavie, and I'll follow," she replied abruptly, but not ungraciously.

As she strolled downstairs she noticed Alison Clarke standing rather aimlessly on the landing, as if she did not quite know where to go or what to do. Dorothy's conscience gave her a prick. She had quite forgotten Alison, who, as a new girl, must be feeling decidedly out of things at the College. She certainly might have employed the eleven-o'clock interval much more profitably in befriending the new-comer than in mooning round the playground by herself, brooding over her own troubles. However, it was not too late to make up for the omission.

"Hallo!" she exclaimed. "Not a very breezy occupation to stand reading the Sixth Form timetable, is it?"

"I've nothing better to do," replied Alison, whose rosy face looked a trifle forlorn. "I don't know a soul here yet, or the ways of the place."

"You know me! Come along to the gym.; we're going to have a committee meeting."

Alison brightened visibly.

"What's the meeting about?" she asked, as she stepped briskly with Dorothy along the passage.

"It's our 'Dramatic'. You see, we who stay for dinner get up little plays among ourselves. Each Form acts one or two every term. They're nothing grand—not like the swell things they have at the College Dramatic Union— and we only do them before the other girls in the gym., but they're great fun, all the same."

"I love acting!" declared Alison, with unction.

"Ever done any?"

"Rather! We were keen on it at the school I went to in Leamstead. I was 'Nerissa' once, and 'Miss Matty' in *Scenes from Cranford*, and 'The March Hare' in *Alice in Wonderland*. I have the mask still, and the fur costume, and Miss Matty's cap and curls."

"Any other properties?"

"Heaps—in a box at home. There are Miss Matty's mittens and cross-over, and her silk dress."

"Good! I must tell the girls that. We requisition everything we can. Where are they having the meeting, I wonder? Oh, there's Mavie beckoning to us near the horizontal bar!"

The day boarders belonging to the Upper Fourth were collected in a corner of the gymnasium, waiting impatiently for a few last arrivals. They made room for Dorothy and Alison, and as Annie Gray followed in a moment or two, the meeting began almost immediately. Hope Lawson, by virtue of her Wardenship, took the chair. The first business of the society was to choose a secretary.

"I beg to propose Dorothy Greenfield," said Grace Russell, putting in her word before anyone else had an opportunity, and looking at Ruth Harmon.

"And I beg to second the proposal," said Ruth, rising to the occasion.

Nobody offered the slightest opposition, and Dorothy was elected unanimously. Very much surprised, but extremely pleased, she accepted the notebook and stump of pencil that were handed her as signs of office.

"The next thing is to choose a play," said Hope, "and I think we can't do better than take one of these *Scenes from Thackeray*. *Miss Pinkerton's Establishment for Young Ladies* is lovely."

"Who'd be Miss Pinkerton?"

"It depends on the costume. She ought to have curls, and a cap and mittens, and a silk dress."

"Can we fish them up from anywhere?"

"Didn't you say you'd had them for Miss Matty?" whispered Dorothy to Alison; adding aloud: "This new girl, Alison Clarke, has the complete costume at home, and she's accustomed to acting. I say she'd better take Miss Pinkerton."

"One can't give the best part to a new girl," objected Annie Gray.

"It's not the best part; it's nothing to Becky Sharp."

"Well, it's the second best, anyhow."

"Oh, never mind that! Let her try. If you find she can't manage it, you can put in somebody else instead. Give her a chance to show what she can do, at any rate," pleaded Dorothy.

"We'd destined Miss Pinkerton for you," murmured Grace Russell.

"Then I'll resign in favour of Alison. Let me take Miss Swartz, or one of the servants—I don't mind which."

It was characteristic of Dorothy that, having reproached herself for neglecting Alison, she was at once ready to renounce anything and everything for her benefit. She never did things by halves, and, considering that she had made a promise in the train, she meant to keep it; moreover, she had really taken a fancy to the new-comer's beaming face.

"So be it!" said Hope. "Put it down provisionally—Miss Pinkerton, Alison Clarke. Now the great business is to choose Becky. Oh, bother! There's the dinner bell! It always rings at the wrong minute. No, we can't meet again at two, because I have my music lesson. We must wait till to-morrow."

Dorothy escorted her protégée to the dining-room, and, when dinner was over, spent the remaining time before school in showing her the library, the museum, and the other sights of the College.

"You don't feel so absolutely at sea now?" she enquired.

"No, I'm getting quite at home, thanks to you. It's such a comfort to have somebody to talk to. Yesterday was detestable."

At three o'clock the Upper Fourth had a literature lesson with Miss Tempest. It was held in the lecture hall instead of their own classroom, and just as the girls were filing in at the door, Dorothy made the horrible discovery that in place of her Longfellow she had brought an English history book. It was impossible to go back, for Miss Pitman was standing on the stairs.

"What am I to do?" she gasped. "How could I have been so idiotically stupid?"

"Can't you look on with somebody?" suggested Alison, who was walking with her.

"Miss Tempest will notice, and ask the reason. She's fearfully down on us if we forget anything. I'm in the front row, too, worse luck!"

"Then take my Longfellow and give me your History. Perhaps I shan't be asked to read. We'll chance it, anyhow," said Alison, changing the two books before Dorothy had time to object.

"No, no; it's too bad!" began Dorothy; but at that moment Miss Pitman called out: "What are you two girls waiting for? Move on at once!" and they were obliged to pass into the lecture hall and go to their seats.

Fortune favoured them that afternoon. Miss Tempest, in the course of the lesson, twice asked Dorothy to read passages, and completely missed out Alison, who sat rejoicing tremulously in the back row.

"You don't know from what you've saved me," said the former, as she returned the book when the class was over. "I should have been utterly undone without your Longfellow."

"It's like the fable of the mouse and the lion," laughed Alison. "I must say I felt a little nervous when Miss Tempest looked in my direction. I thought once she was just going to fix on me. All's well that ends well, though."

"And I won't be such a duffer again," declared Dorothy.

"Mother, dearest," said Alison Clarke that evening, "I didn't think the College half so horrid to-day as I did yesterday. I like Dorothy Greenfield, she's such a jolly girl. She took me all round the place and showed me everything, and told me what I might do, and what I mustn't. We went to the Dramatic meeting—at least, it wasn't the real College Dramatic, but one in our own Form—and I got chosen for Miss Pinkerton. Dorothy's going to be Miss Swartz, I expect. We've arranged to travel together always. She's going to wave her handkerchief out of the window the second the train gets to Latchworth, so that I can go into her carriage; and we shall wait for each other in the dressing-room after school."

"I thought she looked a nice girl," said Mrs. Clarke. "She has such a bright, intelligent face, and she answered so readily and pleasantly when I spoke to her. I'm glad to hear she took you under her wing, and showed you the Avondale ways. You'll soon feel at home there now, Birdie."

"Oh, I shall get along all right! Miss Tempest is rather tempestuous, and Miss Pitman's only tolerable, but the acting is going to be fun. As for Dorothy, she's ripping!"

CHAPTER V
A LITERATURE EXERCISE

The fickle goddess of fortune, having elected to draw together the lives of Dorothy Greenfield and Alison Clarke, had undoubtedly begun her task by sending the latter to live near Coleminster. Mrs. Clarke told all her friends that it was by the merest chance she had seen and taken Lindenlea. She had decided that the climate of Leamstead was too relaxing; and when, on a motor tour with a cousin in the North, she happened to pass through the village of Latchworth, and noticed the pretty, rambling old house to let on the top of the hill, she had at once insisted upon stopping, obtaining the keys, and looking over it. And she had so immediately and entirely fallen in love with its pleasant, sunny rooms and delightful garden that she had interviewed the agent without further delay, and arranged to take it on a lease.

"It's the very kind of place I've always longed for!" she declared—"old-fashioned enough to be picturesque, yet with every modern comfort: a good coach-house and stable, a meadow large enough to keep a Jersey cow in, a splendid tennis court, and the best golf links in the neighbourhood close by. Another advantage is that Alison can go to Avondale College. The house is so near to the station that she can travel by train into Coleminster every day, and return at four o'clock. I'm never able to make up my mind to spare her to go to a boarding school; but, on the other hand, I don't approve of girls being taught at home by private governesses. The College exactly solves the problem. No one can say I'm not giving her a good education, and yet I shall see her every day, and have her all Saturday and Sunday with me. It's no use possessing a daughter unless she can be something of a companion, and I always think Nature meant a mother to bring up her own child, particularly when she's a precious only chick like mine."

Alison had no memory of her father, who had died in her infancy. Her mother had been as both parents to her, and had supplied the place of brothers and sisters as well. Poor Mrs. Clarke could not help fussing over her one treasure, and Alison's education, amusements, clothes, and, above all, health, were her supreme interests in life. The girl was inclined to be delicate; she had suffered as a child from bronchial asthma, and though she had partly outgrown the tendency, an occasional attack still alarmed her mother.

It was largely on Alison's account that Mrs. Clarke had taken Lindenlea. She thought the open, breezy situation on the top of a hill likely to suit her far better than the house at Leamstead, which had been situated too close to the river; and she knew that the neighbourhood of Coleminster was considered specially bracing for those troubled with throat or chest complaints. At fourteen Alison was one of those over-coddled, petted, worshipped only daughters who occasionally, in defiance of all ordinary rules, seem to escape becoming pampered and selfish. She had a very sweet and sensible disposition, and a strong sense of justice. In her heart of hearts she hated to be spoilt or in any way favoured. She would have liked to be one of a large family, and she greatly envied girls with younger brothers and sisters to care for. Dearly as she loved her mother, it was often a real trial to her to be idolized in public. She was quick to catch the amused smile of visitors who listened while her praises were sung, and the everlasting subject of her health was discussed; and to detect the disapproval with which they noticed her numerous indulgences. She felt it unfair that strangers, and even friends, seemed to consider her selfish for receiving all the good things showered upon her. She could not disappoint her mother by refusing any of them, though she would gladly have handed them on to someone less fortunate than herself. To her credit, she never once allowed her mother to suspect that this over-fond and anxious affection made her appear singular, and occasionally even a subject of ridicule among other girls. She submitted quite patiently to the cosseting and worrying about her health, only sighing a little over the superfluous wraps and needless tonics, and wishing, though never for less love, certainly for less close and fretting attention.

Perhaps as the direct result of this adoration at home, Alison was a pleasant companion at school, quite ready to give up her own way on occasion, and enjoying the sensation of sharing alike with everyone else. She was soon on good terms with her classmates, for she was merry and humorous as well as accommodating. Her friendship with Dorothy increased daily. As they travelled backwards and forwards by train together they were necessarily thrown much in each other's company, and they earned the nicknames of "David" and "Jonathan" in the Form.

The contrast between the circumstances and the upbringing of the two girls could not, however, have been stronger. Miss Sherbourne, in adopting Dorothy, had undertaken a charge that was a heavy if self-imposed burden upon her small means. Rigid economy was the rule at Holly Cottage; no luxuries could be afforded, and pleasures were mostly of a kind that did not involve any great expenditure. It was rarely that Aunt Barbara indulged herself even to the extent of a concert ticket or a piece of new music. A fresh piano was out of the question, so she managed to coax a good deal of melody from the old one. If it had not been for the help of her writing she could not have sent Dorothy to the College, and, as it was, such extras as dancing lessons were impossible.

Though Dorothy clearly understood the necessity for economy, she often secretly chafed against it. She was a girl who liked to shine before her schoolfellows, and she felt keenly that she lacked their advantages. It was hard, when all were talking of a play or an exhibition, to have to confess that she had not been, and to hear the others say pityingly: "Why, Dorothy, you never go anywhere!" Her clothes, made by Aunt Barbara at home, though beautifully neat and quite sufficient for a schoolgirl, could not compete with the pretty dresses worn by many of her companions; and she did not possess even a watch, much less bangles and chains such as Hope Lawson was fond of displaying.

The knowledge of her dependent position, which Aunt Barbara had so carefully kept hidden, came to her as the most serious of her drawbacks. She could not help brooding over it, and the more she dwelt upon the subject the more disconsolate and discontented she became. Aunt Barbara, whose loving eyes were quick to notice, saw only too clearly the phase through which Dorothy was passing; but she knew that the girl must fight her own battle before she learnt to set the right value on this world's possessions, and to discover for herself what things are really of worth. With Dorothy's character Miss Sherbourne often felt as though she were working in the dark. She did her best to impress her own personality upon the child, but every now and then some unexpected trait—a legacy, perhaps, from an unknown ancestor—would crop up and make her realize how strong is the force of heredity in our natures. She recognized that at the present crisis "preaching" would be useless, and could only trust that patience and forbearance would indirectly bring about the desired effect.

"Auntie," said Dorothy, as she ate her breakfast one morning, about a month after the term began, "I don't like Hope Lawson since she got the Wardenship. She hasn't improved."

"How's that? I thought she was a tolerably nice girl," answered Miss Sherbourne.

"She wasn't at all bad before, but she's changed. She and Blanche Hall and Irene Jackson go together now, and they simply sit upon all the rest of the class."

"Rather a large order, if they do it literally!" laughed Aunt Barbara.

"Metaphorically, of course. But really, Auntie, you've no idea how nasty they are. Hope has taken the tone that she's much above everyone else—I don't mean because she's Warden, but socially. You see, while her father has been Mayor they've entertained numbers of distinguished people, and Hope's never tired of talking about them. Then she comes to school wearing heaps of bangles and rings and things, and she makes one feel she doesn't consider one's clothes anything to hers. She saw my blue skirt had been lengthened, for she nudged Irene and laughed, and said very pointedly that braid had gone out of fashion. Then she asked me where I bought my boots. I wasn't going to tell her, so I didn't answer; but Blanche Hall piped out: 'The Market Stores', and they both screamed with laughter, and Hope said she always bought hers at Forster's."

"I should simply take no notice, if I were you."

"I try not to, but all the same it's annoying. Yesterday we had a squabble about giving out the French books, and I said I should ask Miss Pitman; then Hope said Miss Pitman would be sure to take her part, because she often dines at their house. And the worst of it is, it's true. Miss Pitman isn't quite fair. Hope and Blanche and Irene make the most tremendous fuss of her, and she always favours them—she does really. She gives them better marks for their exercises, and easier questions in class, and waits much longer for their answers than for anybody else's. She doesn't like me."

"Dorothy!"

"She doesn't—honestly, Auntie. Even Alison notices how down she is on me. If I do the least little thing I'm snapped up in a second."

"Then the obvious moral is, don't do the least little thing."

Dorothy pulled a long face.

"Auntie! You were brought up by a private governess, and you don't know what it is to go to a huge school. One can't always be absolutely immaculate; if one could, one would be a saint, not an ordinary girl. I can't resist talking sometimes, or shuffling my feet, or fidgeting with my pencil, or—no, no; if you're going to lecture, I shall fly! It's ten past eight, and it's too wet to take the short cut across the field."

Dorothy certainly considered she had a grievance at present. She had unfortunately not made a very good impression upon her new teacher. She could not bear to curry favour, and, seeing that Hope and some of the others were trying by every means in their power to pay special court to Miss Pitman, she went to the opposite extreme, and became so abrupt as to be almost uncivil in her manners.

"I'm not going to bring her flowers every morning, and offer her walnut creams in the interval," she thought. "It seems like bribery, and I should think much better of her if she wouldn't accept them. Miss Hardy never did."

Miss Hardy, the mistress of the Lower Fourth, had been strict but scrupulously just; she might be sometimes disliked by her pupils, but she was always respected. Miss Pitman was a totally different type of teacher: she was younger, better looking, dressed more prettily, and cared very much more for the social side of life. She lacked power to enforce good discipline, and tried to supply her deficiency by making a bid for popularity among her girls. She dearly loved the little attentions they paid her: she liked to pin a rose on her dress, or carry home a bunch of hothouse flowers; she found tickets for concerts or lectures most acceptable; and invitations—provided they were to nice houses—were not despised. Probably she had not the least idea that she was allowing her predilection for some of her pupils to bias her judgment of their capacities in class, but in the few weeks that she had taught the Upper Fourth she had already gained a reputation for favouritism.

"She can be so particularly mean," said Dorothy, continuing the recital of her grievances to Alison in the train. "She deliberately helped Blanche out with one question yesterday, and she wouldn't give me even the least hint."

"I don't like her myself," commented Alison, "though she isn't as hard on me as she is on you. But it's perfectly easy to see what's the matter with Miss Pitman—she's ambitious to climb. She wouldn't accept the Parkers' invitation (they only live in a semi-detached villa), and she's been twice to the Lawsons', who send her home in a motor. Well, she won't be asked to our house."

"Nor to ours, though I don't suppose she'd want to come. All the same, it's disgusting, and I've a very poor opinion of her."

That morning Miss Pitman took her classes without her ordinary adornment in the way of a button-hole. Hope Lawson was absent, and the delicate Maréchal Niel or dainty spray of carnations that usually lay on her desk at nine o'clock was absent also. Perhaps she missed it, for she was both impatient and snappy in her manner during the lessons, waxed sarcastic when Noëlle Kennedy demanded an explanation of a rather obvious point, and made no allowance for slips. She dictated the History notes so quickly that it was very difficult to follow her, and woe to Dorothy, who was rash enough to ask her to repeat a sentence!

"Are you deaf, Dorothy Greenfield? Sit up and don't poke. I can't allow you to stoop over your desk in that way. If you're shortsighted, you had better go to an oculist and get fitted with glasses."

Dorothy was apt to poke, and her attitude when writing was most inelegant; but it is difficult to remember physical culture during the agonies of following a quick dictation. She frowned and looked thunderous as she made a jerky effort to sit straight.

"Miss Pitman's crosser than usual," she said to Alison at eleven o'clock. "You'll see, I shall only get 'Moderate' for my literature exercise, however well I do it."

"You mean she'll mark it low on purpose?"

"Yes; she never judges me fairly."

"But does she look at the names on the labels when she's correcting?"

"You may be sure she does, or Hope wouldn't always have 'Very Good'."

"Then, just as an experiment, let us exchange. I'll write my exercise in your book, and you can write yours in mine. Our writing's sufficiently alike."

"Oh, that would be a gorgeous joke! We'll do it; but don't tell a soul. Let us go upstairs and arrange it now."

Dorothy wrote her literature exercise that morning in the book labelled "Alison Clarke". She had prepared her subject carefully, and did her very best not only to put down correct facts, but to attend to points of composition. She tried to avoid tautology, unduly long sentences, and various other mistakes to which she was prone, and flattered herself at the end of the half-hour that she had turned out a decidedly creditable piece of work. She blotted it with great satisfaction, and by rather officiously collecting the books of several girls who sat near, and placing hers in the middle of the pile, she managed to hand it to the monitress without showing the incriminating "Alison Clarke" on the cover. There was a singing class from 12 to 12.45, during which time Miss Pitman always did her corrections. When the girls rushed up to the classroom at a quarter to one, the books were finished and placed ready upon the table. Alison and Dorothy each seized her own, and retired together to a corner of the room.

"You've got 'Fair' in my book," whispered Dorothy. "Now let me see what I've got in yours."

"'Excellent'!"

"Fiddlesticks!"

"Well, look for yourself."

"It actually is! Oh! Miss Pitman would never have given me 'Excellent' if she'd known it was mine. I feel I've scored no end. Doesn't it show her up?"

"Rather!"

"Excellent" was the very highest mark possible, and it was rarely given at the College. To receive it was certainly a great honour, and showed the merit of the exercise. The two conspirators thought they had been extremely clever, and congratulated themselves upon the success of their little plot; but it was to have a sequel which neither of them expected in the least. Miss Tempest taught literature throughout the school, and though she delegated the correction of exercises to assistant mistresses, she occasionally made some enquiry about the written portion of the work. That afternoon she entered the Upper Fourth classroom.

"I wish to know the results of your literature exercises," she announced. "I myself set the paper this week, and I want to see what standard you have reached individually. Will each girl in turn repeat her mark, beginning with Noëlle Kennedy?"

Dorothy was in a quandary: she did not know what she ought to say. Must she give the mark that was written in her book, or the one she had really gained? Justice seemed to point to the latter, so when it came to her turn she answered "Excellent". Alison, taking the cue from her, answered "Fair". Evidently the exercises had not reached a very high standard of merit that day. There were a few "Goods", a great many "Moderates" and "Fairs", and even one or two "Weaks" and "Faulties". At the end of the recital the head mistress was just about to give her comment, when Miss Pitman intervened.

"May I say a word, Miss Tempest? One girl has not stated her mark correctly. Dorothy Greenfield said 'Excellent'. Now I particularly remember that I only gave one 'Excellent' this morning, and that was not to Dorothy."

Miss Tempest turned to Dorothy with her sternest look.

"Repeat your mark!" she ordered.

"Excellent," quavered Dorothy, sticking to her point, though she foresaw a storm.

"Hand me your exercise!"

Dorothy fumbled in her desk with trembling fingers. She knew she was involved in a most awkward situation. She was very pale as she passed up the book. Miss Tempest opened it and glared first at the "Fair", written plainly in Miss Pitman's handwriting, and then at the embarrassed face of her pupil.

"I should not have thought you would consider it worth while to attempt to deceive me with so palpable a falsehood, Dorothy Greenfield!" she said scornfully.

Dorothy turned all colours. For once her wits deserted her. She could not imagine how to explain the matter. The whole thing had happened so suddenly that there seemed no time to cudgel up a word in self-defence. A groan of indignation passed round the class, which Miss Tempest instantly suppressed.

"Well, what have you to say for yourself, Dorothy? Do you consider such conduct worthy of a girl who was nominated for the Wardenship?"

"Please, Miss Tempest, may I speak?" said a voice at the back; and Alison Clarke stood up, blushing scarlet, but determined to have her say.

"Do you know anything about this, Alison?"

"Yes; it's my fault. We changed exercise books. The one in Dorothy's book marked 'Fair' is really mine, and here is Dorothy's, marked 'Excellent', in my book. If you'll please look at it you'll see it's her own writing—she makes Greek e's, and I never do."

Miss Tempest frowned, but she nevertheless examined the exercise, which a row of eager hands passed up to her.

"Is this Dorothy Greenfield's writing, Miss Pitman?" she asked.

"It certainly has all the characteristics," admitted the Form mistress.

"Why were you writing in each other's book?" enquired Miss Tempest sharply.

Alison's scarlet face took an even deeper shade of crimson.

"Oh—just silliness!" she murmured. "But it seemed more honest each to take the mark we'd really gained. I couldn't give in 'Excellent' when I'd only had 'Fair'."

"Take care such a thing never happens again," said Miss Tempest, eyeing both the culprits, who at that moment would have given a great deal to have been a little less clever. "You will each put down 'Fair' in your reports."

"So I've lost my 'Excellent'," lamented Dorothy after school. "Miss Pitman will be rejoicing; I believe she 'twigged'."

"I'm almost certain she did, she was looking at you so keenly. Well, there's one good thing, it will show her that we think she favours."

"Much she'll care!"

"Oh, I don't know! No teacher likes to be accused of unfairness."

"I know one thing—I should have got into an uncommonly big scrape if you hadn't put in a word."

"Well, it was much easier for me than for you, as you'd got the 'Excellent'."

"But I haven't got it now, worse luck! And probably I shan't have another all this term," groaned Dorothy.

CHAPTER VI
A PROMISE

Dorothy had grown so accustomed to travelling to school with Alison that she felt extremely at a loss when one morning she looked out of the carriage window at Latchworth and did not see the familiar rosy, smiling face on the platform.

"I wonder if Alison's late, or if she's stopping at home?" she thought. "She had rather a cold yesterday, and Mrs. Clarke seems so fearfully fussy. I'm glad Aunt Barbara doesn't worry over me to such an extent; it must be a perfect nuisance to have to wear galoshes just on the chance of its raining, and to swathe a Shetland shawl over your mouth if there's the slightest atom of damp in the air. And Alison is so conscientious over it! I believe I should stuff the shawl inside my satchel, and lose the galoshes on purpose!"

The journey seemed dull without her friend and their usual chat together. It was not interesting to stare out of the window when she knew every yard of the line by heart, and for lack of other occupation she was reduced to taking out her books and looking over her lessons. Both in the mid-morning interval and the half-hour before dinner she missed Alison exceedingly. She tried to fill up the time with various expedients. She got a book from the library, and was so long and so fastidious in choosing that the prefect in charge grew tired of recommending, and waxed impatient.

"Really, Dorothy Greenfield, you might be a literary critic! One is too childish, and another's too stiff, and you don't care for historical tales. I should like to know what you do want! Be quick and take something, or I shall just lock the case up again and leave you without anything. Oh, you'd like *The Old Curiosity Shop*! Then why couldn't you say so at first?"

Though Dorothy had settled on a Dickens for the sake of making some choice, she had no intention of reading just at present, and she sauntered into the gymnasium to see what the others were doing. It was not the day for a dramatic rehearsal, and nothing particular was going on. Some of the girls were playing rounders, but most were standing about chatting, and waiting for the dinner bell. Hope Lawson and Blanche Hall were talking together, and as Dorothy passed she caught a fragment of their conversation.

"We shall have to fly, the second dinner is over," said Hope; "but I believe we shall just be able to do it."

"If we only get a peep at the dresses as they go in, it will be worth it," replied Blanche. "I hear there are to be twelve bridesmaids and two pages. We'll do a bolt!"

"What are Hope and Blanche talking about?" said Dorothy to Addie Parker, who was standing close by.

"Why, there's a grand wedding at St. Peter's at two o'clock. Miss Russell is to be married, and I suppose it will be ever such a swell affair. They were laying down red carpets when I passed this morning. I peeped into the church, and some men were just bringing pots of the loveliest flowers."

"Are Hope and Blanche going to see it, then?"

"Yes, no doubt. Bertha Warren and I mean to go, and so do Annie Gray and Joyce Hickson. I wouldn't miss it for the world. You'd better come."

"I'll think about it," returned Dorothy.

The more she considered the idea the more she liked it, in spite of the fact that it was a rather doubtful adventure. There was no exact rule that the girls should not leave the College during the dinner hour, but it was well understood, all the same, that they remained on the premises.

"Miss Tempest has never said so," thought Dorothy, "nor have any of the mistresses. When a thing hasn't been forbidden, I suppose it's allowed. St. Peter's is just round the corner, so I declare I'll go. I've never seen a smart wedding."

As soon as dinner was over she fled to the dressing-room to put on her outdoor clothes, then, as Blanche described it, she "did a bolt". She much preferred going by herself to joining Addie Parker and Bertha Warren, so she scurried along, hoping they would not overtake her. At the lich-gate of the church she came upon Hope Lawson and Blanche Hall.

"Hallo, Dorothy! So you've sneaked away too?" said Hope.

"I don't call it sneaking," returned Dorothy. "Why shouldn't we come?"

"Yes, why shouldn't we, indeed?" echoed Blanche.

"No reason at all, my dear," observed Hope, "except that Miss Tempest might happen to make a bother about it if she heard. One never knows quite what she'll take it into her head to say or do."

"Then she mustn't hear."

"Right you are! We certainly won't tell of each other."

"Rather not!"

"Will you promise too, Dorothy, never to breathe one single word that you've seen Blanche and me here?"

"Of course! Do you think I'm likely to go telling tales to Miss Tempest?"

"Well, no; but you'll promise not to tell any body, not even the girls?"

"All serene!"

"On your honour?" said Hope, catching her by the arm.

"On my anything you like," answered Dorothy, who, seeing Bertha Warren and Addie Parker coming up, was in a hurry to get away.

She was anxious to try to obtain a place in the church, so that she might see something of the ceremony. All the seats seemed taken as she entered, but she marched confidently up the aisle, hoping to find room farther on. She was stopped directly, however, by the verger.

"What name, please? Are you one of the Miss Guntons?" he enquired.

"No," stammered Dorothy, "I—only——"

"Then you must go out," he interrupted tartly. "These pews is for the invited guests—general public's only allowed in the free seats, and they're full up long ago."

Much abashed, Dorothy beat a hasty retreat, after having caught a brief vision of elegantly-dressed guests and beautiful rows of palms and chrysanthemums in pots. Evidently there was no room for schoolgirls. She was annoyed with herself for having ventured there. Her pride hated rebuffs, and the old verger's manner made her feel hot and uncomfortable. Several people in the pews had turned to look at her. No doubt they considered her an impertinent intruder. Her cheeks flamed at the idea. The churchyard seemed almost as full as the church, though the crowd there was of a totally different description. The possibility of witnessing the wedding had attracted a motley assemblage—nurses with babies and small children, errand boys, hatless women from back streets, dressmakers' assistants who had come to see the fashions, and a number of those idlers who are always to be found ready to run and look at anything in the way of a show, be it a marriage, a funeral, or an accident.

By a little judicious elbowing, Dorothy managed to secure a place where she had a tolerable view of the path and the lich-gate. She was wedged rather tightly between two nursemaids, and the basket of a grocer's boy behind was pressing into her back; but these were minor discomforts, which must be endured.

"Here they come!" said somebody.

There was a rustling and swaying movement among the crowd, a sound of carriage wheels, a general craning forward of heads; the nurse next to Dorothy held up her little charge in her arms. It was difficult to see, for the awning rather hid the view from those in the churchyard above the path. All that Dorothy caught was a glimpse of a figure in white satin and lace, and just a peep of some bridesmaids in palest blue; then a tall woman moved in front of her, and effectually shut out the prospect.

"What a swindle!" she thought. "I've hardly seen anything at all. It wasn't worth the trouble of coming. I wonder if the other girls have had better luck?"

She noticed two school hats in the distance, though she could not recognize the faces under them. She was half inclined to struggle through the groups of people towards them, when she remembered to look at the church clock.

"Nearly twenty-five past!" she ejaculated. "I must fly!"

It was not an easy matter to extricate herself from the crowd. Dorothy knew it was useless to attempt to go out by the main entrance, so she made a push for the side gate; then taking a short cut by a small street, she scurried back to school. She was just changing her boots in the dressing-room when Addie Parker, Bertha Warren, and three other girls came hurrying in.

"Oh, Dorothy! Did you get off?" cried Addie. "You are lucky! We were all caught!"

"Yes, caught dead—every one of us!" echoed Bertha.

"Oh, it was horrible!" exclaimed Joyce Hickson. "I never expected she'd be there."

"And we ran almost plump against her!"

"Just our luck!"

"What do you mean? Who caught you?" asked Dorothy.

"Miss Tempest. Didn't you see her?"

"No, not I."

"Then thank your good star!"

"Where was she?"

"Close to the lich-gate. She came up quite suddenly, just when the bride had gone in. Phyllis saw her first, and passed on a 'Cave', but it was impossible to get away, there were so many people round."

"She must have noticed our school hats in the distance," added Annie Gray.

"What did she do?" asked Dorothy.

"Pulled out her notebook and took all our names. Oh, I'm just shaking in my shoes! I didn't know whether I dared come back to school, or whether I hadn't better trek straight off home."

"You'd have got into a worse pickle still if you'd done that."

"Perhaps I should. Anyhow, I'm quaking."

"Yes, it's 'Look out for squalls'!"

"Squalls? A tempest, you mean!"

"It will be a raging Tempest, certainly."

"Oh, goody! There's the bell, and I haven't changed my boots!"

"Did you see anything, though?" asked Dorothy, as they hurried upstairs.

"Yes, I had a lovely view. The bridesmaids were sweet; their bouquets were all of lilies of the valley: and as for Miss Russell—it makes me want to be married myself! It was almost worth while being caught to see it—but oh, dear! what will happen to us, I wonder? I'd give everything I possess to have this afternoon over."

Full of uneasy forebodings, the delinquents took their places at their desks. Dorothy looked round for Hope and Blanche. They slipped in at the last moment, rather red and out of breath, and seemingly anxious to avoid the enquiring eyes of the others.

Miss Carter, the science mistress, entered, and the hygiene lesson began. Eight guilty souls in the class found it difficult to fix their attention upon ventilation or food values. Dorothy's mind was in a ferment. What was about to happen? She had not thought it any great crime to go to see the wedding, but apparently such an action was viewed far more seriously at head-quarters. In her speculation on the issue of events, she gave such random answers that Miss Carter stared at her in surprise.

"Did you misunderstand the question, or are you not attending, Dorothy Greenfield?" she asked.

Dorothy made an effort to pull herself together and recall the forgotten facts, but they were elusive, and she could only stare stupidly at the teacher. Just at that moment the door opened, and Miss Tempest entered. There was a perceptible shudder amongst those girls whose consciences told them they were to blame. Addie Parker and Bertha Warren exchanged glances, Joyce

Hickson pretended to be absorbed in her notebook, while Hope Lawson sat with her nose in the air, as if unconscious of any need to disturb herself.

"Excuse me for interrupting the lesson, Miss Carter," began Miss Tempest, "but there is a very important matter upon which I must speak at once. Adeline Parker, Bertha Warren, Joyce Hickson, Annie Gray, and Phyllis Fowler—stand up!"

With downcast eyes the five girls responded to the command.

"I wish to know what you were doing at St. Peter's Church this afternoon?"

No one had the courage to venture a reply.

"Who gave you permission to leave the school?"

Still there was dead silence among the culprits.

"You know perfectly well the day boarders are not allowed to go out during the dinner hour."

Miss Tempest's voice, which had begun icily, was waxing more stern and wrathful. Addie Parker began to sob.

"How is it that among all the girls at the College you five had the presumption to attempt such a flagrant breach of the rules? I say you five, for I saw you and took your names; but I certainly noticed another Avondale hat among the crowd, and I intend to find out to whom it belonged. Was any other girl in this class present at St. Peter's this afternoon?"

Dorothy's conscience gave a great, uncomfortable prick. She had many faults, but concealment was not one of them, so she stood up.

"I was there, Miss Tempest," she said, rather defiantly.

At the head mistress's gaze Dorothy dropped her eyes. Miss Tempest was not to be trifled with.

"Indeed! By whose permission?"

"I didn't ask anybody. I didn't know the dinner girls weren't allowed to go out. We none of us knew. We thought we had a perfect right to go."

"That cannot be true. You have been four years at the College, and no one is better acquainted with the rules than yourself. It is an unheard-of thing for day boarders to leave until four o'clock, and could not be allowed for an instant. I am astonished that you should commit such a breach of discipline and then attempt to justify yourself—yes, astonished and disappointed in the extreme."

"But I really didn't——" began Dorothy.

"That will do," interrupted Miss Tempest sharply. "I don't wish to hear any further excuses. You have shown me that you are not to be trusted."

"But I do speak the truth!" burst out Dorothy.

"Dorothy Greenfield, if you answer me back again, I shall have to request you to leave the College altogether. I do not allow any girl to set her opinion against mine."

When Miss Tempest was angry, her mouth looked grim and her eyes blazed. Quite cowed, Dorothy did not venture to seek further to exculpate herself. She stood twisting her hands nervously, and (I regret to say) with a very stubborn expression on her face. Inwardly she was raging. The head mistress glared at her for a moment, then turned to the class again.

"Was any other girl in this room at St. Peter's this afternoon?" she asked. "I appeal to your honour."

Nobody answered. Hope and Blanche sat still, with eyes that dared not raise themselves to meet those of the mistress.

"Very well; I am glad to find no others have broken the rule. For the rest of the term the six girls who so forgot themselves will not be allowed in the gymnasium between one and half-past two. If it is too wet to go into the playground, they must stay in the classrooms. Any of the six who enters the gymnasium during the prohibited time must report herself to me at once in the library. Thank you, Miss Carter. I am sorry to have been obliged to disturb your lesson, though more sorry still for the cause of the interruption."

Dorothy took in very little of the remainder of the hygiene lesson. She was in a ferment of indignation. Miss Tempest had doubted her word before all the Form, and that rankled more than the scolding. Her contempt for Hope and Blanche was supreme, but she was angry, all the same, at their meanness. She was far too proud to cry like Addie Parker, whose eyes were already red and swollen, and whose cheeks were blotched with tears. She sat, a sullen, defiant little figure, nursing her wrath and full of a burning sense of injustice.

Fortunately, the rest of the afternoon was devoted to drawing, and she was able to give a mechanical attention to her copy, which made her work just pass muster.

"Not so good as usual to-day, Dorothy," said the art mistress at the close of the class. "I can only give you 'Fair'. I don't think you have tried your best."

Dorothy shut her pencil box with a slam. She was in a thoroughly bad temper, and felt that she did not much care what happened. Miss Giles gave her a warning look, as if she were disposed to tell her to lose an order mark; but seeing perhaps that the girl was overwrought and unlike herself, she took no further notice, and passed on to the next drawing board.

As Dorothy left the studio, Hope Lawson managed to edge close up to her, and whispered in her ear: "Remember your promise! You said you wouldn't tell a soul—not even one of the girls."

"You don't deserve it," mumbled Dorothy.

"But you promised on your honour—if you have any honour. Perhaps you haven't."

"I've more than you," retorted Dorothy. "You and Blanche are a couple of sneaks. There! you needn't look so aghast. I'm not going to blab. I've enough self-respect to keep a promise when I've once made it, though, as I said before, you don't deserve it. You the Warden, too! A nice example you are to the Lower School, if they only knew it!"

"They mustn't know it. Promise me again, Dorothy; promise me faithfully you won't tell. I'll bring you a huge box of chocolates if you'll keep this a secret."

"I don't want your chocolates!" said Dorothy scornfully. "I've told you already that I don't break my promises. You're safe enough as regards me."

"Silence!" called the mistress; and the two girls fell into line again as they marched with their drawing boards down the corridor.

In the dressing-room the rest of the Form had plenty to say about the occurrence.

"You've done for yourself, Dorothy," declared Ruth Harmon. "You'll be in Miss Tempest's bad books for evermore."

"I can't see that I was any worse than the others," snapped Dorothy; "not so bad, indeed, because I wasn't caught, and yet I owned up. Miss Tempest might have taken that into account."

"She would have, I dare say, if you hadn't answered her back," said Noëlle Kennedy.

"I only told her I didn't know we mightn't go."

"But you said it so cheekily, and Miss Tempest hates cheek above everything. I shouldn't care to be in your shoes now. What a good thing you weren't chosen Warden!"

Dorothy tugged at her boot lace till it snapped, then had to tie the two ends together in a knot. How hard it was to keep her unwelcome secret! She felt as if in common justice the girls ought to be made aware of the moral cowardice of their leader.

"I'd have made a better one than some—yourself not excepted," she growled.

"My lady's in her tantrums to-day," chirped Ruth.

"I'm not! What a hateful set you all are! I wish to goodness you'd leave me alone!"

Dorothy seized her books and stalked away without a good-bye to anybody. How thankful she was that Avondale was a day school, and that she could shake the dust of it from her feet until nine o'clock to-morrow morning!

"If I weren't going home to Aunt Barbara now, I should run away," she thought. "It would be dreadful to have to endure this all the evening. Oh dear, I hate the place, and I hate Miss Tempest, and I hate the girls, and everything, and everybody!"

Poor Dorothy carried a very sore heart back to Holly Cottage that evening, but she cheered up when she entered the pretty little sitting-room, with its bright fire and a cosy tea laid ready on the oak table. After the storms and whirlwinds of school, home seemed such a haven of refuge, and Aunt Barbara—who always understood—so utterly different a personality from Miss Tempest.

"I'm cross and horrid and disagreeable and altogether fractious, Auntie!" she said, squatting on the hearthrug after tea, with one of the dear hands squeezed in hers, while she poured out her accumulation of troubles. "I've got to keep that promise, but I can't do it with any good grace, and I still feel that Miss Tempest was unjust, because nobody had ever said we mightn't leave the Coll. in dinner-time. And I'm barred the gym. It's too disgusting, because it puts me out of all rehearsals, and I shall have to give up my part in the act."

"Poor old sweetheart, you've certainly been in the wars to-day! But honestly, don't you think it is just the least little scrap your own fault? I fancy at the bottom you knew that dinner girls aren't expected to run out into the town whenever they like, even to look at weddings—and it wasn't justifiable to speak rudely to Miss Tempest, was it?"

Dorothy stared hard at the fire.

"No; I suppose I was cheeky. Auntie, when I'm at school and things are horrid, I just flare up and explode—I can't help it. I'm quite different at home. I wish I had lessons with you again, like I did when I was a little girl. I'd be far nicer."

"A soldier isn't good for very much until he's tried, is he? School is your battlefield at present, and the temper is the enemy. Won't you be a Red Cross Knight, and ride out to do full and fair fight with it? It's as ugly a dragon as ever attacked St. George."

"And a great deal harder to conquer, because every time I kill it, it comes to life again, ready for another go at me. There, Auntie! yes, I'll make a try; but I know I shall do lots more hateful things—I always do!"

CHAPTER VII
ALISON'S HOME

Dorothy was ready enough at making good resolutions—the difficulty always lay in keeping them when they were made. At night in bed it would seem fairly simple to practise patience, forbearance, charity, humility, and many kindred virtues, yet the very next morning she would come down to breakfast with a frown that caused Aunt Barbara to sigh. Full of high ideals, she would dream over stories of courage and fortitude till she could believe herself ready to accomplish the most superhuman tasks and overcome innumerable difficulties. She always hoped that when she was grown up she might have a chance of emulating some of her book heroines, and doing a golden deed which the world should remember. In the meantime many little ordinary, commonplace, everyday duties were left undone. She was not thoughtful for others, and was content to let Aunt Barbara do everything for her, without troubling herself to consider what she might offer in return.

Miss Sherbourne was not blind, and saw only too clearly that the girl was passing through a selfish phase.

"I've seen it often enough in others of her age," she thought. "They are so sweet while they are little children, and then suddenly they lose all their pretty, childish ways, and become brusque and pert and uncompromising. I suppose they are struggling after their own individualities and independence, but it makes them ruthless to others. At present Dorothy is rather inclined to rebel against authority, and to assert herself in many directions. She needs most careful leading and management. She's affectionate, at any rate, and that's something to go upon."

Aunt Barbara could not guess all the trouble that was in Dorothy's mind. Though the latter had never referred again to the story of her adoption, the fact that she was a foundling continually rankled. She was so sensitive on the point that she imagined many allusions or slights which were not intended. It was extremely silly, but when the girls at school talked about their brothers and sisters, she often believed they did so purposely to make her feel her lack of relations. If two friends whispered together, she would think they were speaking of her; and any small discourtesy, however unintentional, she put down as an indication that the others considered her inferior to themselves. She contrived to make herself thoroughly miserable with these ideas, and they had the unfortunate effect of causing her to be even more abrupt and brusque than before. Sometimes one traitor thought would even steal in, and she would question whether Aunt Barbara really loved her as truly as if she had been her own flesh and blood; but this was such a monstrous and unjust suspicion that Dorothy would thrust it from her in horror at having ever entertained it.

One pleasure that she had at Avondale was her friendship with Alison Clarke. Owing to their daily companionship in the train, she had managed to keep Alison pretty much to herself, and she watched over her with jealous eyes, unwilling to share her with anybody else. Alison had been away from school on the day that the truants went to the wedding, and it was nearly a week before she returned. Each morning Dorothy had looked out for her at Latchworth, and every time she had been disappointed. At last, however, the familiar little figure appeared again on the platform, and the round, rosy face smiled a greeting.

"No, I've not been very ill—only a bad cold. It's almost gone now. Oh, yes, I'm delighted to go back to the Coll. It's so dull staying in the house with nothing to do except read, and one gets sick to death of chicken broth and jelly! I want somebody to tell me school news. It seems more like a year than a week since I stopped at home."

Dorothy was accommodating in the matter of news, and the two chattered hard all the way to Coleminster.

"It's a fearful nuisance you're out of rehearsals," said Alison. "Can't we all come up to the classroom and have them there instead?"

"No; Miss Pitman won't let us. We six sinners are on penance; we mayn't do anything but read. Oh, it's disgusting! I shall be out of the Christmas performance altogether."

"No, you shan't," declared Alison; "not if I can compass it in any way."

She said no more just then, but when they were returning in the train that afternoon she mentioned the subject again.

"I was talking to the girls at dinner-time," she began. "We were planning out the programme. Really, the scene from *Vanity Fair* is very short. Hope says it won't take as much time as the play you had last year, so I suggested that we should have some tableaux as well. You could do characters in those without any rehearsing. What do you think of my idea?"

"Ripping!" said Dorothy. "We haven't had tableaux at the Coll. for ages. But we must manage to get hold of some decent costumes."

"I've heaps and heaps in a box at home," announced Alison complacently. "I can lend them all. We'll get up something worth looking at. Tell me what you'd like to be, and you shall have first choice of everything."

"It depends on what there is."

"There's a lovely mediaeval dress that would do for Berengaria of Navarre."

"She had golden hair, and mine's brown!"

"Bother! so she had. Then that's off. Never mind, there are heaps of others. There's a Cavalier's, if it will only fit. I wonder if it's big enough? You'd look nice with the crimson cloak and huge hat and feather. Or there's a Norwegian peasant's—I think the skirt would be long enough—and a Robin Hood jerkin and tall leather boots. I believe you could wear them. Oh dear! you ought to try all the things on. I wish I could show them to you. They're kept in an oak chest on the landing."

"I should like to see them," said Dorothy pensively.

"Then look here! Get out with me at Latchworth and come to our house. Mother has gone to Bardsley this afternoon and won't be home till seven, so I shall be quite alone. You'd have heaps of time to come, and catch the next train on to Hurford."

It was a most tempting proposal. Dorothy wanted immensely to go. She knew she was expected to come straight home from school every day, and not to accept any invitations without permission, but she dismissed that remembrance as inconvenient.

"Auntie'll only think I've missed the train. It will be all right if I catch the next," she reasoned. "One must have a little fun sometimes, and I'm getting too old to have to ask leave about everything. All right, I'll come," she added aloud; "I'd just love to see those costumes."

It was delightful to get out of the train with Alison and walk to the house on the hill which she had so often admired from the carriage window. Dorothy was in wild spirits, and made jokes till Alison almost choked.

"It makes me cough to laugh so much," she protested. "Do be sensible, Dorothy! Here we are. Leave your books and your umbrella in the porch. We'll go straight upstairs."

Dorothy could not help looking round with interest as her friend led her up the staircase. At every step her feet sank into the soft carpet.

Through an open door she could catch a glimpse of a beautiful drawing-room, and beyond was a conservatory full of flowers. On the landing, which surrounded the hall like a gallery, were marble statues, pictures, and inlaid cabinets; and the floor was spread with Turkey rugs. From the window she could see a tennis lawn and a vinery. After the modest proportions of Holly Cottage, it all seemed so spacious and handsome that Dorothy sighed.

"What a lovely house to live in!" she thought. "Alison is lucky. She's no foundling. I wish I had half her things. I wonder why some girls have so much more than others?"

Quite unconscious of the storm of envy that she had roused, Alison walked on. She was so accustomed to her surroundings that it never struck her how they might appear to anyone else, and her sole thought was of the tableaux.

"Here's the chest," she cried, lifting the lid in triumph, and commencing to pull out some of the dresses. "This is the Norwegian peasant's—I knew it was on the top. Let me try the skirt by yours. Oh, it is too short after all! Then you must have the mediaeval one. Look! Isn't it a beauty?—all trimmed with gold lace and spangles."

Dorothy examined the costume with appreciation, but shook her head ruefully.

"You don't imagine that would meet round my waist?" she enquired. "It looks about eighteen inches. For whom was it made?"

"Mother, before she was married. I always tell her, girls must have been like wasps in those days. Try the Cavalier's. Oh, I don't believe you can wear that either! You're so big! I wish I could lop a little off you. Can't you possibly squeeze into this?"

"I would if I could, but no—I'm several sizes too large. Haven't you anything else?"

"Not so nice. These are quite the best. You see, they're made of really good materials, and the others are only of glazed calico and sateen. I'll tell you how we'll manage. We must put several costumes together. Take off your coat and hat and I'll show you. Now, if you have the mediaeval dress on first, we can tuck the bodice inside, and drape the Cavalier's cloak like a pannier to cover the waist. The Norwegian bodice goes quite well with it, and that's big enough, at any rate. Now this gauze scarf round your shoulder, and this big hat, and there you are. Oh, it's lovely!"

"What am I intended to be?" asked Dorothy, looking down at her miscellaneous finery.

"A Venetian lady in the time of the Doges. It is after the picture in the drawing-room. Oh, it is like! It's simply splendid—you've no idea how good!"

"What picture?"

"The portrait of Aunt Madeleine in fancy dress. Why, Dorothy, you're just the living image of it! Come downstairs at once and let me show you. It's perfect."

Quite carried away by her own enthusiasm, Alison dragged Dorothy along the landing, the latter much encumbered by her long skirt and the necessity for holding on most of the articles of her attire.

"Don't go so fast," she implored; "I'm losing the pannier, and the hat's nearly bobbing off. If you'll hold the train behind, I may manage better."

"All right; but then I can't see you—the back view isn't nearly so nice. This way—I have to steer you like a ship. Here's the drawing-room. Now, take a good look in the glass first, and then please admire the picture."

The face that greeted Dorothy in the mirror was the prettiest version of herself that she had ever seen. The quaint costume, the scarf, and the big hat suited her admirably; the excitement and fun had brought unwonted roses to her cheeks, and her eyes were as bright as stars. She had had no idea that it was possible for her to look so well, and the surprise heightened the colour which was so becoming.

"Now the picture—look straight from yourself to the picture!" commanded Alison.

The portrait hanging on the opposite wall was that of a young lady of perhaps seventeen. The face was pretty, with grey eyes and regular features; the splendid Venetian dress set off to advantage the dark curls and the graceful turn of the neck; the slender hands held a lute, and the lips looked as if they had just closed after finishing the last refrain of a song. Whether it was the effect of the costume or not, there certainly was some resemblance between the face in the painting and that of the girl who was scrutinizing it. Dorothy could see that for herself, though the likeness did not seem so striking to her as it appeared to her friend.

"You're the absolute image!" declared Alison. "It might have been painted directly from you. Bruce!" (to a servant who was crossing the hall) "Bruce, come here! I want you to look. Did you ever see anything so exact? Isn't she Aunt Madeleine to the life?"

Bruce gazed contemplatively from the painted face to the living one.

"The young lady certainly favours the picture," she said. "I suppose it's the dress, and the way her hair's done. Miss Alison, your tea's ready. I've put it in the library this afternoon."

"Then bring another cup. Dorothy, you must stay and have tea with me. Yes, you must! You don't know how I hate being alone, and Mother won't be home till seven. Oh, do, do! You can't think how much I want you."

"But I shall miss the 5.30!"

"Never mind, you'll get the next train. Isn't there one at six? Bruce, fetch the railway guide please. Oh, thanks! Now then, Coleminster to Hurford— where are we? Latchworth—yes, there's one at 6.5. Dorothy, you'll have oceans of time. I can't let you go without tea."

It seemed a pity, when she was there, not to stay, so Dorothy argued. Of course, Aunt Barbara would be getting rather anxious, but her mind would soon be set at rest afterwards, and Dorothy was not given to troubling very much about other people's fears.

"It's twenty-five past now," she said, looking at the Sèvres clock that stood on a bracket. "I should have a fearful rush to catch the 5.30."

"You couldn't do it, so that settles the matter. Take off your costume and come to the library. Oh, never mind folding the things up; Bruce will do that. Leave them anywhere."

A dainty little tea awaited the girls in the library, an attractive room to Dorothy, with its bookcases, filled with beautifully-bound volumes; its big lacquered cabinet, and the many curios and Eastern weapons that adorned the walls.

"Where do all these things come from?" she asked, gazing round with interest while Alison wielded the teapot.

"Most of them are from India. My father was out there. Uncle David is at Delhi still, only perhaps he's coming home next year for good. Aunt Madeleine died at Madras."

"The one in the picture?"

"Yes; she and Uncle David had only been married quite a short time. She was Mother's twin sister; but they weren't the least scrap alike—Aunt Madeleine was dark, and Mother is so very fair. Wasn't it funny for twins? You're far more like Aunt Madeleine than Mother is. That's quite absurd, isn't it?"

"Quite," agreed Dorothy.

"Uncle David sends me such lovely presents from India," continued Alison, who liked to talk when she could find a listener. "I've all sorts of little scented boxes and things carved in ivory. I simply must show some of them to you. I'll get them in half a second," and away she fled, returning to spread the table with her treasures.

To Dorothy the meal was a mixture of cake, filigree ornaments, blackberry jam, and sandalwood boxes.

"I wish we had some of the roseleaf preserve left," remarked Alison. "It was the queerest stuff— rather too sickly, but I should like you to have tasted it; it came from Kashmir. Look here, I want to give you one of these boxes; yes, you must take it! I've so many others, and I'd love you to have it. I'm going to put it in your pocket, and I shall be very offended if you take it out."

Alison crammed the box into Dorothy's pocket as she spoke. It was the greatest pleasure to her to give a present, and she would willingly have bestowed far more of her treasures if she had thought there was a likelihood of their being accepted. She had enough delicacy and tact, however, to understand that her proud little friend would not care to be patronized, so she restrained her generosity for the present.

"It's so delightful to have you here!" she continued. "Wouldn't it be lovely if you could come for a whole Saturday, or to stay the night some time? I'm going to ask Mother to ask you. We'd have such a jubilee! Can you play poker patience? Oh, I love it too! And I've the sweetest wee packs of cards you ever saw. I want to show you my stamps and my crests. I've got two big books full, and some are really rare ones. I'll bring the stamps now."

"Alison, I simply can't stay!" exclaimed Dorothy. "Look at the time! Why, I shall just have to race to the station!"

"Oh, bother! Yes, you'll have to fly. I always allow five minutes. I've never tried running, because Mother says I mustn't—it makes me cough. Where are your hat and coat? Why, of course, we left them on the landing. You haven't finished your cake— —"

"Never mind!" cried Dorothy, who was already out of the door and hastening upstairs to fetch her outdoor garments. "Oh, it's been so jolly to come and see you, Alison! I have enjoyed it. Just hold my coat—thanks. I'm putting on my hat wrong way about! Bother! I'll alter it in the train. Where are my satchel and umbrella? Good-bye; I shall just have to sprint."

Alison stood looking regretfully down the drive as her friend hurried away. She was loath to part with her, and turned indoors with a sigh. She dearly loved young companions, and the beautiful house and its many treasures seemed dull without a congenial soul of her own age with whom to "go shares". She was full of Dorothy's visit when her mother returned home, and poured out a most excited and rather jumbled account of it.

"It just suddenly occurred to me to ask her, you know, Mother, because I did so want her to try on those costumes. She put on the mediaeval one, and the Cavalier's cloak and hat, and the Norwegian bodice, and then she looked exactly like the picture of Aunt Madeleine. Wasn't it queer?"

"I dare say the combination of costumes made quite a good copy of the Venetian dress," responded Mrs. Clarke.

"But it wasn't the dress that was so like—it was Dorothy. You never saw anything so funny, Mother! She was the absolute image of the portrait—far more like than I am to you. Even Bruce saw it."

"You take after your father, not me."

"I don't know who Dorothy takes after, and I don't suppose she does either. She's never seen her father or mother. She doesn't even know who they were. Isn't it horrid for her?"

"How is that?"

"Oh, it's quite romantic! Some of the girls at school told me, but I daren't say a word about it to Dorothy, she's so proud and reserved. I never even hint at it. Miss Sherbourne—that's her aunt—at least, not her real aunt—oh! I'm getting muddled—well, Miss Sherbourne found her in the train when she was a baby—there was a dreadful railway accident at a place called Greenfield, and that's why she's called Dorothy Greenfield—but it isn't her proper name, because they don't know that—they never found out who she was—and Miss Sherbourne adopted her, and Dorothy always calls her Auntie, though she's no relation at all. And Hope Lawson says Dorothy's a charity child, and her parents may have been quite poor; but I'm sure she's a lady, because—well—because she somehow seems to have it in her. I think she's just lovely, and I like her better than anyone else at school."

"Where did you hear this amazing story, Birdie?" exclaimed Mrs. Clarke.

"I told you, Mother dear—at the Coll. All the girls know about it. They call Dorothy 'The Foundling' behind her back. Nobody dares to say it to her face, because she gets into such tantrums. I think it makes her so interesting. She may be the daughter of a nobleman, for what anyone knows. Just imagine! Suppose she found out that her father was a duke! Then she'd be Lady Dorothy. Don't you think, Mother, she looks aristocratic? I do."

"I think you're a very silly child," returned Mrs. Clarke, with a distinct tone of annoyance in her voice. "You must not bring girls to the house without asking me first."

"But, Mother darling, you weren't in this afternoon, and I'd thought of the tableaux, and I couldn't arrange any of the parts until I knew what dresses would fit Dorothy. I simply had to get her to come and try them on. And it was such fun having her to tea. Mayn't I ask her to spend the day here next Saturday? Oh, and if you would let her stay until Monday, we'd have such a glorious time!"

"Certainly not; I couldn't think of such a thing," replied Mrs. Clark decisively.

"But, Mother—Mother dearest—why not? You said yourself what a nice girl she looked that first day we saw her in the train, and how glad you were that I had her to travel to school with."

"That was quite a different matter."

"But why shouldn't I have her to the house? Oh, Mother, I told Dorothy that I meant to ask you to invite her, and if you don't I shall feel so silly. What could I say to her? Mother sweetest, please, please!"

"You have no right to give invitations without consulting me first, Birdie," said Mrs. Clarke, who looked more displeased than her daughter remembered ever having seen her before. "I cannot allow you to make friends with girls of whom I know nothing."

"But you'd know her if she came here, Motherkins."

"I don't wish to—nor do I want you to continue the acquaintance. No, Birdie, it is impossible. I absolutely forbid you to ask this Dorothy Greenfield here again."

It was the first time Mrs. Clarke had ever set her will in direct opposition to Alison's, and the spoilt child could hardly realize that she was not to be allowed, as usual, to do as she liked. She burst out into a final appeal.

"But, Mother, I love Dorothy! We're always together. You don't know what chums we are at school. If you only guessed half of how much I want it, you'd say yes."

"But I say no, Birdie," answered Mrs. Clarke, firm for once in her life. "I strongly discourage this acquaintance, and you must not be more friendly with Dorothy than you can help. I prefer you to travel to school in another carriage."

"How can I? What explanation could I possibly give? It would seem so peculiar to cut her for no reason at all."

"I suppose you will have to be civil, but you must not be intimate. You are to see no more of her than you can help. It is very annoying that she goes by the same train. In such a large school as Avondale there are surely plenty of other and more suitable girls with whom you can make friends."

"Not one so nice as Dorothy," gulped Alison, beginning to cry. "If you'd only ask her, and see for yourself!"

"Birdie, I don't want to be cross with you, but you must understand, once and for all, that I will not have this girl at the house. No, I shall not explain; it is quite enough for you that I forbid it. Don't mention the subject to me again."

Alison ran upstairs in floods of tears. She could not understand why her mother had taken this sudden prejudice against Dorothy. The thought of breaking off the friendship was misery to her; added to this, she was so used to getting her own way that it seemed strange to have any reasonable request refused—and she considered this one to be most reasonable. In matters of health she was accustomed to obey, to submit to be wrapped up in shawls, to put on galoshes, to be kept in bed and dosed and dieted; but where her health was not concerned she had almost invariably been consulted, and her wishes gratified. It was the first time her mother had ever flatly refused to listen to her coaxings, or had spoken to her with the least approach to severity, and such a state of affairs was as unpleasant as it was unusual.

"She really meant it, too," sobbed Alison. "Oh, dear! What am I to do? Dorothy'll think me such an atrocious sneak!"

CHAPTER VIII
A SHORT CUT

When Dorothy left Lindenlea she had exactly three minutes in which to catch her train. Her long legs raced down the drive and along the road to the station. Panting and out of breath, she rushed up the incline to the little gate. The train had come in; she could see the smoke from the engine. It generally only waited for about a minute, but there was still time to get in, if she were extremely quick.

"Ticket, please," said the collector at the gate.

"Contract!" cried Dorothy, trying to rush past; but the man put out his arm to bar the way.

"Show it, please; I must see all contracts," he said curtly.

Chafing at the delay, Dorothy felt in her pocket; then to her dismay she remembered that she had left her contract at home. The officials at Hurford and Coleminster knew her so well by sight that when once they had seen her season ticket on the first day of the term, they never asked to look at it again, but simply let her pass unchallenged. As she was not required to produce it daily, she had grown careless, and often forgot to take it with her. The collector at Latchworth had not seen her before, and of course could not tell that she possessed a season ticket at all.

"I've left it at home, but it's a contract between Hurford and Coleminster. You'll find it's quite right. Please let me through. I must catch this train," she urged.

"Can't let anyone pass without a ticket," answered the man. "If you haven't your contract you must book an ordinary fare. Booking office is round that corner."

Dorothy stamped with impatience.

"I haven't any money with me, and there isn't time either. Let me pass, quick! The train's going!"

In reply, the man shut the gate and locked it.

"Can't let anybody on to the platform when the train's in motion. You'll have to wait till the eight o'clock now," he observed, with aggravating calm.

On the outside of the railing, Dorothy almost wept with rage. To see the train steaming out of the station without her was too exasperating. There would have been quite time to catch it if the collector had not been so full of "red tape" notions. She felt angrier than she could express, especially at the cool way in which the man had told her to wait till eight o'clock. Eight o'clock! It was impossible. Why, Aunt Barbara would think she was lost or stolen! She was late enough as it was, and other two hours would be dreadful. Then, again, there was the question of her ticket. The official evidently would not accept her word for the contract if she could not produce the actual piece of pasteboard, and she had no money to book with. Should she run back to Lindenlea and ask Alison to lend her the fare? No; Mrs. Clarke might have returned by now, and it would make such a fuss. Dorothy always hated to ask favours, or put herself in a false position. She felt that to turn up at the house again, wanting to borrow a few pence, would be a most undignified proceeding, and would exhibit her in an unfavourable light to her school-mate's mother.

"I'd rather walk home than do that," she said to herself.

The idea was a good one. Why should she not walk home? It was only about four miles, and she would arrive at Hurford much sooner than if she waited for the train. To be sure, it was growing very dusk, but she was not in the least afraid. "I'm perfectly capable of taking care of myself," she thought. "If I met a tramp and he attacked me, I'd belabour him with my umbrella. But I've nothing on me worth stealing; my brooch is only an eighteenpenny one, and I don't possess a watch."

Dorothy generally made up her mind quickly, so without further delay she walked down the station incline and turned on to the high road that led to Hurford. She had soon passed through the straggling village of Latchworth, where lights were already beginning to appear in cottage windows, and labourers were returning home from work. As she passed the last little stone-roofed dwelling she looked back almost regretfully, for it seemed like leaving civilization behind her. In front the road stretched straight and white between high hedges, without ever a friendly chimney to show that human beings were near.

Dorothy suddenly remembered all the tales that Martha had told her, in her childhood, of children who were stolen by gipsies and carried away in caravans to sell brooms or dance in a travelling circus. She knew that Martha had rubbed in the moral so as to deter her from straying out of the gate of Holly Cottage when she was left to play alone in the garden, and that the stories were probably made up for the occasion—Dorothy at fourteen did not mean to be frightened, as if she were seven—but, all the same, the old creepy horror which she used to feel came back and haunted her. The road was so very lonely, and it was growing dark so fast! Suppose a gipsy caravan appeared round the next corner, and a dark, hawk-visaged woman were to demand her hat and jacket! What would she do? The supposition made her shiver. She walked on steadily all the same, her footsteps sounding loud in her ears.

Then she stopped, for in front of her she heard the unmistakable creak of a cart. Was it a band of gipsies or travelling pedlars? At school, in daylight, she would have mocked at herself for having any fears at all, but now she found her heart was beating and throbbing in the most absurd and uncomfortable fashion. "I'm in a horrid scare," she thought. "I daren't meet whatever's coming, and that's the fact. I'm going to hide till it's passed."

There was a gate not very far away; she managed to open it, and crept into a field, concealing herself well behind the hedge. The creaking came nearer and nearer. Through a hole Dorothy could see down into the roadway. By a curious coincidence, it was a caravan that was passing slowly in the direction of Latchworth; the outside was hung with baskets, and there was a little black chimney that poured out a cloud of smoke. Two thin, tired horses paced wearily along, urged by an occasional prod with a stick from a rough-looking boy. A swinging lantern under the body of the vehicle revealed a couple of dogs, and in the rear slouched three men and a slipshod, untidy woman, who twisted up her straggling hair as she went. Hidden behind the hedge, Dorothy watched them go by.

"I'm most thankful I came up here and didn't meet them," she thought. "They look a disreputable set. I believe they'd have stolen anything they could lay hands on if they'd realized I was alone. I expect I've had quite an escape. I wonder if that's the whole of the tribe, or if there are any more caravans?"

The idea of more was discomfiting, yet it was possible that this was only the first of a travelling company. Dorothy remembered that there were some wakes at Coleminster about this time every year, which would no doubt attract van-dwellers from many parts of the country. To meet a succession of these undesirables along the road would be anything but pleasant. Yet what could she do? She certainly did not want to turn back either to the station or to Lindenlea. Time was passing rapidly, and she must push forward if she did not wish to be caught in the dark. Then she remembered that Martha had once spoken of a short cut between Hurford and Latchworth. Martha walked over occasionally on Sunday afternoons to see a cousin who lived in Latchworth village, and she had given a minute description of the route. Dorothy recollected quite well that, starting from Hurford, the maid had crossed some fields, gone through a wood, and come out by a path that led through a small, disused quarry on to the high road. She had said it cut off a long corner, and saved almost a mile.

"If I can only find the quarry," thought Dorothy, "I'll try that short cut. I don't suppose I can go wrong if I follow the path through the wood. I shall be glad to get off the road, at any rate."

The caravan had passed out of sight, so she came down from her hiding-place and hurried on in search of the quarry. She had not walked very far before she found it—a craggy little ravine, with heather growing over the rocks, and heaps of stones and shale lying about. This must surely be the place, so she turned at once off the high road into it. There was not a soul about. Some agitated blackbirds, annoyed at her vicinity, went fluttering out of the bushes, tweeting a warning to other feathered friends; and something small—either a rat or a rabbit—scuttled away into the grass and dried fern in a great panic at the sight of her. The sun had set some time ago, and the last tinge of red had faded from the sky. The grey, chilly dusk was changing from a neutral tint to black. A landscape on an evening at the beginning of November is never very cheerful, and Dorothy felt the depressing influence of the scene. The few wind-swept trees at the head of the ravine stretched long, bare branches, which looked like fingers prepared to clutch her as she passed. The grass was damp and sodden, and here and there a pool of water lay across the path. She was quite glad when she was out of the quarry, and found herself in an open field. It was a comfort to see the sky all round, even though the light was failing.

"I'm sure it's grown dark to-night much quicker than it did yesterday," she exclaimed. "How fearfully overcast it is, too! I believe there'll be rain in a few minutes. Here's the wood. It looks quite thick and fairy-tale-y—the sort of place to meet a giant or an ogre!"

A stile led from the field into the wood. Dorothy scrambled over, and began to follow a path through the trees. It was very dark indeed, for most of the oaks still kept their leaves, and shut out the little remaining light overhead. She could just see to stumble along, and had the greatest difficulty to trace her way. It was wet under foot; the ground was marshy in places, and strewn with dead leaves. After a little while she came to a place where the path seemed to branch in two directions. Which to choose she could not tell; both seemed equally bad and indistinguishable. Reckoning that Hurford must lie to the left side of her, she turned to the left, almost feeling her way among the trees.

"If I don't get out of the wood soon, I shan't be able to see at all. I hope it's not far," she thought. The path grew a trifle better; there were a few stones put down on it. Was she at last coming to a stile? What was that dark patch in front of her? She stopped short suddenly, drawing back just in time to avoid stepping into water. Why, it must be a well! It was a deep pool, edged round with stones, and with a hedge of holly surrounding it on three sides.

Perhaps the path led by the back of it. No; the bushes were so thickly matted with a tangle of brambles that it would be impossible to push through. Evidently the path only led to the well, and she must have taken the wrong turning where it had branched. Almost crying, she began to retrace her steps, and hurried faster and faster through the gathering darkness. She was back at last at the spot where she had made the mistake, and this time she turned to the right. The trees seemed to be even nearer together than before, and there was a thick undergrowth which sent out long blackberry trails that caught and tore her coat as she scurried by. She had slung her school satchel on her back, and as she ran it bumped her shoulder almost like somebody hitting her from behind.

IN DISCREET HIDING

It grew so dark at last that Dorothy stopped in despair. It seemed absolutely impossible to find her way, and the horrible truth dawned upon her that she was lost—lost as thoroughly and effectually as any knight of romance; while it seemed extremely unlikely that she would find the convenient pilgrim's cell or hermit's cave that generally turns up in story-books to shelter the adventurer. To add to her misery, the rain that had been threatening for some time came on, and descended in a torrent. She put up her umbrella and sheltered herself as well as she could behind a tree, but her boots and skirt were already sopping with wet. She felt chilly and cold, and her spirits had descended to the very lowest ebb. Would she be obliged to stay there the whole night, until it was light enough to find her way? The prospect was appalling.

"What a horrid pickle and hobble I've got myself into!" she thought. The rain came down faster than ever, and suddenly there was a vivid streak of lightning and a loud crash of thunder. Dorothy screamed aloud, for thunder held terrors for her; yet even in the midst of her fright there was a grain of comfort—the bright flash had lit up the wood like an electric lamp, and had shown her, almost within a few yards, the stile for which she was seeking. Off she went in the direction where she had seen it, groping her way anyhow, and tearing her clothes on thorns and brambles.

She seemed to have arrived at a hedge, and she began to feel her way along it carefully, hoping to reach the stile. At last her hand touched a wooden bar; it was either the stile itself or a hurdle, she did not care which, if only she could climb over. It looked equally dark, however, on the other side; and even if she got into the field how was she ever to find the path to the high road? At this juncture she saw a small, rather flickering light moving through the gloom a little distance off. It must be a lantern, she thought; and whether the bearer were poacher, gipsy, or thief, she would summon him to help her out of her difficulty. She gave a lusty shriek, and went on calling at the top of her voice. The lantern stopped still for a moment, then, to her intense joy, began to move in her direction. At first she could see nothing but a yellow ring of light, then she made out a dark figure behind; and presently, as it came quite near, she recognized the ruddy face and stubby grey beard of Dr. Longton, who lived in Hurford village, nearly opposite the church. Dorothy's amazement at seeing the doctor was only equalled by his astonishment at finding her in such a predicament.

"My blessed child! What are you doing here?" he exclaimed.

"Oh, Dr. Longton, I'm so thankful it's you! I was sure you were a tramp, or a poacher, or somebody dreadful!" cried Dorothy hysterically.

"Nothing half so interesting; only a common or garden practitioner coming back from visiting a patient," he laughed. "You haven't told me what you're doing here. Give me your hand, and I'll help you over the fence."

"Trying to find a short cut, and losing my way," confessed Dorothy. "I thought I'd have to spend the night in the wood."

"A very unpleasant camping ground at this time of year! I've slept under the stars myself once or twice, but not in November. That was a loud peal of thunder! I think the storm's passing over—the rain has almost stopped."

With his lantern to guide them, the doctor escorted Dorothy to the door of Holly Cottage, and said good-bye with a twinkle in his eye.

"I won't ask inconvenient questions, but it strikes me you've been up to something, you young puss!" he said. "Take my advice, and stick to the 4.30 train in future. If your aunt scolds you, tell her I say you deserve it!"

Aunt Barbara did not scold—she was too relieved at her bairn's safe return to do anything except welcome and cosset the prodigal; but the look in her sweet eyes hurt Dorothy more than any reprimand.

"I didn't know she cared so much as that," thought the girl. "I won't stop away another time, not for a thousand invitations. It isn't the horrid walk, and getting lost, and the darkness, and spoiling one's clothes I mind, it's—well—oh, Dorothy Greenfield, you're a nasty, thoughtless, selfish wretch to make Aunt Barbara look so, and if you do such a thing again I shan't be friends with you any more—so there!"

CHAPTER IX
DOROTHY SCORES

Dorothy and Alison met next morning with a shade of embarrassment on either side. Dorothy was a little ashamed of herself for having accepted her friend's invitation without leave from Aunt Barbara, and not particularly proud of her experiences on the way home. She had at first been inclined to tell Alison about her adventure; then she decided it would be rather humiliating to have to explain that she had forgotten her contract, that she had had no money in her pocket, and that the official had not seemed disposed to trust her for her fare. Alison, whose path in life was always smooth, would perhaps scarcely understand the situation, and it might not reflect altogether to her own credit. Therefore, she did not even mention that she had missed the 6.5 train, and after a hurried greeting buried herself in her books, trying to gather some idea of her lessons, which had been much neglected the night before.

Alison, on her side, was relieved that Dorothy did not refer to her visit to Lindenlea. She was most anxious to avoid the subject of her invitation; she felt it would be extremely awkward to be obliged to tell Dorothy point-blank that her mother refused to endorse it: and, mindful of the prohibition against too great intimacy, she left her schoolfellow to her books, and made no advances. The two walked from the station to the College almost in silence, each occupied with her own thoughts; and though they met frequently during the day, and travelled back together as usual, they only talked about ordinary Avondale topics. Each felt as warm towards the other as before, but both realized that theirs must be a friendship entirely confined to school, and not brought into their home lives. Dorothy, though she was far too proud to hint at the matter, easily divined that Mrs. Clarke had disapproved of Alison's action in taking her to the house, and that she did not mean to give her any future invitation. That hurt her on a sore spot.

"She thinks me a nobody!" she groaned to herself. "If I had been Hope Lawson, now, or even Val Barnett, I'm sure I should have been asked. Alison hasn't even mentioned the tableaux again. I suppose she's not allowed to lend me the costume. Well, I don't care; I'll wear something else."

But she did care, not only about this, but about many things that happened in class. It is not pleasant to be unpopular, and in several ways Dorothy was having a hard term. Hope Lawson, who had never been very friendly at any time, seemed to have completely turned against her, and was both supercilious and disagreeable. Hope did not like Dorothy, whose blunt, downright ways and frank speech were such a contrast to her own easy flippancy. Money, position, and pretty clothes were what Hope worshipped, and because Dorothy possessed none of these she looked down upon her, and lost no opportunity of slighting her. In her capacity of Warden, Hope naturally had much influence in the class, and led popular opinion. It was very unfortunate that she had been elected, for she was quite the wrong girl to fill a post which involved a tolerable amount of moral responsibility. The tone of a Form is a subtle, intangible thing; it means certain codes of schoolgirl honour, certain principles of right and wrong, certain standards of thought and views of life, all of which need keeping at a high level. Under Hope's rule the Upper Fourth began to show a general slackness; rules were evaded where possible, work was shirked, and a number of undesirable elements crept in.

Though Hope, to curry favour, made a great fuss of Miss Pitman to her face, she was not loyal to her behind her back. She would often mimic her and make fun of her to raise a laugh among the girls. Hope encouraged the idea that a mistress was the natural enemy of her pupils, and that they were justified in breaking rules if they could do so safely. She did not even draw the line sometimes at a "white lie"; her motto was, "Keep pleasant with your teacher on the surface, but please yourself when she can't see you, and do anything you like, so long as you're not caught".

One morning when Dorothy came into the classroom, she found Hope seated on her desk, exhibiting a new ring to a group of admiring friends. Dorothy paused a moment, then, as nobody moved, she protested:

"I'll thank you to clear off. I want to get to my desk."

Hope giggled.

"I'll thank you to wait a little, then. I mean to stay where I am for the present," she said, in a mocking voice.

"But you're on my desk!"

"Well, what if I am? A warden has the right to sit upon anybody's desk she likes."

"Oh, Hope!" sniggered the others.

"What's the good of being Warden if you can't? The post must have some advantages."

"Hope Lawson, do you intend to clear off my desk?" asked Dorothy, with rising temper.

"I don't know that I do, Dorothy—er—I suppose your name is Greenfield?"

"For shame, Hope!" said Grace Russell. "I'm disgusted with you. Why can't you move?"

Grace enforced her words by a vigorous tug, and drew Hope away to her own place. With two flaming spots in her cheeks, Dorothy opened her desk. She was too angry for speech. Grace's compassionate looks hurt her almost as much as Hope's insult. She did not want pity any more than scorn.

"I hardly know a word of the History," Hope was saying. "We had some friends in last night, and we were all playing 'Billy-rag'. Do you know it? It's a new game, and it's lovely. I scarcely looked at my lessons. However, I begged a concert ticket from Father, and brought it for Pittie. It's 'Faust', at the Town Hall, and it's supposed to be tiptop. She'll let me off easy this morning, you'll see."

"Hope, you're not fair!" objected Grace.

"Why not? If Pittie chooses to overlook my lessons on the score of concert tickets, why shouldn't she? She's keen on going to things. Likes to show off her new dresses. I suppose I shall have to get her an invitation to the Mayor's reception. By the by, who's going to the Young People's Ball at the Town Hall? It's to be a particularly good one this year."

"I am, for one," said Val Barnett, "and I think a good many of the Form will be there. Helen Walker, and Joyce Hickson, and Annie Gray are asked, I know."

"Are you going, Dorothy?" enquired Hope, with a taunt in her tone.

"Dorothy never goes anywhere!" laughed Blanche Hall.

Dorothy buried her head in her desk and took no notice; but her silence was pain and grief to her.

"Hope's too mean for anything!" whispered Ruth Harmon to Noëlle Kennedy. "I'm sorry for Dorothy."

"And Pittie's too bad. It's not worth while preparing one's work if Hope gets all the praise for nothing. Why is Pittie always so hard on Dorothy?"

"Oh, because Dorothy doesn't flatter her up; besides, she loves presents. I wonder what she'd say if she could hear what her darling Hope says about her sometimes?"

"I wish she'd find her out."

"She can't, unless someone tells, and I hate sneaks."

"Well, I'm really sorry for Dorothy Greenfield. Hope and her set seem to have taken a spite against her. I don't mind if her dresses are shabby, and if she's the only girl in the Form who doesn't own a watch. I vote we make up a special clique to be on her side."

"All right; I'm your man! I admire Dorothy she's so 'game'—she never gives way an inch, whatever Hope says she just sticks her head in the air and looks proud."

"She flares up sometimes."

"Well, I don't blame her. I like a girl who won't be kept down."

"What could we do to boost Dorothy up a little in the Form? Most of the girls are like sheep; if anyone leads hard enough, they'll follow."

"Well, I've an idea."

"Go ahead!"

"You know Dorothy's splendid at acting. She ought to take a principal part in our Christmas play."

"But she can't rehearse. She's barred the gym. and tied to the classroom for the rest of the term."

"That's my point. I think Dorothy got much too hard a punishment. Miss Tempest was angry because she answered back, and never took into account that she had owned up about going to that wedding, and that it was honest of her to tell."

"Yes, 'The Storm-cloud' was savage because Dorothy was cheeky, but I think she's got over it a little now; she's been far nicer to her lately."

"Have you noticed that too? Well, I believe Miss Tempest knows she treated Dorothy severely, and she's sorry, only she doesn't like to eat her own words. My plan is that we get up a deputation, go to the study, and beg her to let Dorothy off for rehearsals. She knows what a point we make of the play."

"Splendiferous! I verily believe we shall succeed. Shall we go at eleven?"

"No; we must talk to the others first, and get up as big a deputation as we can. The more of us who ask, the better."

The weather, which beforetimes had never troubled Dorothy overmuch, was at present a subject of the most vital importance to her. If it were fine, she might go into the playground at one o'clock; but if it were wet, she was obliged to remain in durance vile in the classroom, while most of the girls were amusing themselves in the gymnasium. On this particular day it poured. Dorothy looked hopelessly out of the window to see the gravelled stretch, where the girls often practised hockey, turned into a swamp, and a river racing under the swings. With a groan she resigned herself to the inevitable. The society of her five fellow-victims was not particularly exhilarating, so she took a library book from her desk and began to read. As a rule, those who were free to do so left the schoolroom only too readily, but to-day Hope Lawson and some of her chums lingered behind. They were in a silly mood, and began drawing caricatures on the blackboard.

"Watch me do Professor Schenk," cried Hope, taking the chalk. "Here's his bald head, and his double chin, and his funny little peaked beard. Do you like it? Well, I'll draw you another. Miss Lawson's celebrated lightning sketches! Who'll you have next?"

"Do Pittie," said Blanche.

"All right; give me the duster and I'll wipe out the Professor. Now then, how's this? Here's her snubby nose, and her eyeglasses, and her fashionable fuzz of hair. She's smirking no end! 'Don't I look nice?' she's saying," and Hope drew a balloon issuing from the mouth of the portrait, with the words "Don't I look nice?" written inside; then, encouraged by the laughter of her friends, she added "G. A. Pitman, otherwise Pittie", over the top.

Dorothy, who wished to read her story, had retired to the extreme back of the room, and sat in a corner, but she nevertheless heard all that was going on.

"Yes, Pittie fancies herself," continued Hope. "You should see what costumes she comes out in for evening wear. I'm sure she's greater on toilet hints than literature."

"How do you make that out?"

"Observation, my dear. If you could look inside her desk, you wouldn't find it full of classical authors; there'd be novels and beauty recipes instead."

"She keeps it locked, at any rate."

"Wise of her, too. If we could only open it now! Hallo! She's actually forgotten to lock it to-day! What a joke! Let us see what she's got here!"

"Particularly honourable for a warden!" came a voice from the other end of the room.

Hope turned round angrily.

"Indeed, Madam Sanctimonious! So you've grown a prig all of a sudden? Who asked Saint Dorothy to interfere?"

"Go on, Hope," said Blanche; "we're not goody-goody."

"Well, I mean to have a look, at any rate. There! Didn't I tell you? The first thing I find is a novel. What a heap of papers! I believe she must keep her love letters here. Oh, girls, I say, here's a portrait of a gentleman!"

Blanche, Irene, and Valentine came crowding round, all sense of honour lost in their curiosity.

"Oh, what a supreme joke!" they exclaimed.

Now the back desks of the classroom were raised on a platform, and in the corner where Dorothy sat there was a tiny window that served the purpose of lighting the passage. From her place Dorothy that moment caught a vision—no less a person than Miss Pitman herself was walking down the corridor. Should she give a warning "Cave!" and let the others know? She was not sure whether they deserved it.

"Look here, you wouldn't be doing this if Miss Pitman could see you!" she remonstrated. "Why don't you stuff those things back and shut up the desk?"

"Shut up yourself, Dorothy Greenfield, and mind your own business!"

"On your heads be it, then," muttered Dorothy. "I tried to save you, but here comes swift vengeance!"

At that moment through the open door walked Miss Pitman. She stopped short and surveyed the scene through her pince-nez. There was her portrait on the blackboard—not at all a flattering one, especially with the inscription issuing from her mouth, but quite unmistakably meant to represent her, for her name was written above. At her open desk were her four favourite pupils, giggling over the photograph which Hope held aloft. It was a disillusionment for any teacher, and Miss Pitman's mouth twitched.

"What are you doing at my desk?" she asked sharply.

No girls were ever so hopelessly caught. Hope remained with the photograph in her hand, staring speechlessly; Blanche tried to shuffle away, Valentine looked sulky, and Irene—always ready for tears—pulled out her pocket-handkerchief.

"Who has drawn this picture on the blackboard?" continued Miss Pitman.

"Hope—Hope did it! It wasn't any of us!" snivelled Irene, trying to thrust the brunt of the affair on to her friend's shoulders.

Miss Pitman gave Hope a scathing glance, under which the girl quailed.

"An extremely clever way of showing her talent for drawing, no doubt," remarked the mistress sarcastically. "I shall be obliged if someone will clean the board."

Several officious hands at once clutched the duster and erased the offending portrait. Miss Pitman walked to her desk, closed the lid, locked it, and put the key in her pocket.

"It is superfluous to tell you what I think of you," she said. "Miss Tempest will have to hear about this."

"Well, Hope's done for with Miss Pitman, at any rate," said Bertha Warren to Addie Parker, when the outraged mistress had taken her departure, and the four sinners had fled downstairs.

"Yes, there'll be no more favouring now—and a good thing, too! It was time Miss Pitman's eyes were opened. Will she really tell Miss Tempest?"

"Serve them right if she does. I'm waiting for developments."

There was not long to wait. At two o'clock, Hope, Blanche, Irene, and Valentine received a summons to the study, and after a ten minutes' interview with the head mistress came away with red eyes.

"Have you heard the news?" said Noëlle Kennedy presently. "There's been a most tremendous storm—a regular blizzard—in the study. Miss Tempest has been ultra-tempestuous, and Hope and the others have come out just wrecks."

"What's the matter?" enquired some of the girls who had not heard of the occurrence in the classroom.

"Hope found Miss Pitman's desk unlocked, and she and Irene and Val and Blanche were calmly turning over the contents when Pittie popped into the room and caught them. Then the squalls began. They had to report themselves in the study, and it turned out that there was something else against Hope and Blanche. I don't know who gave them away, but somebody had been telling Miss Tempest that they were at the wedding that day. She charged them with it, and was simply furious because they hadn't owned up when she asked the class."

"I can tell you who told her," volunteered Margaret Parker. "It was Professor Schenk. He saw them there, and he happened to mention it this morning."

"Well, Miss Tempest was fearfully stern. She said Hope wasn't fit to be Warden, and to represent the Lower School, if she'd no more idea of honour than that. She's taken away the Wardenship from her. She says it's not to be decided by election again—she's going to choose a girl for herself."

"Whom has she chosen?"

"Grace Russell," said Ruth Harmon, who at that moment joined the group. "It's just been put up on the notice board."

"Well, I'm glad. Grace will make a good Warden."

"Yes, there's something solid about Grace. She never lets herself be carried away."

"Hope will be crestfallen."

"Never mind—it will do Hope Lawson good to find she's not the most important person in the Form."

"I say," interposed Noëlle, "isn't this a good opportunity to put in a word for Dorothy? She owned up when Hope didn't, so Miss Tempest ought to remember that. Let us strike while the iron is hot, and go to the study now."

"Right you are! Where are Mavie and Doris? I'm sure they'll come too."

Dorothy's champions walked boldly into the study, and put their case so successfully to Miss Tempest that she condescended to consider it. Perhaps, as Noëlle suspected, she thought she had given too severe a punishment, and was ready to remit it. In the end, she consented to forgive, not only Dorothy, but her companions in misfortune also, granting all six permission to enter the gymnasium again.

"It's a complete turning of the tables," said Ruth, as the girls returned triumphantly from their mission "Dorothy's free, and Hope and Blanche will have to stay in the classroom and do their share of penance."

"Then they'll be out of rehearsals."

"Of course they will."

"And who's to take Becky Sharp?"

"I vote for Dorothy."

"So do I. She deserves it."

"Where is she? Let's take her her order of release."

The events of that day had an effect upon the Upper Fourth in more ways than one. Perhaps Miss Pitman had learnt a lesson, for in future she accepted no presents at all from her pupils, not even flowers, and showed special favour to nobody. The Form liked her much better now that she was more impartial.

"I can't stand a teacher who pets one girl and snubs another," said Ruth. "It isn't just, and one has a right to expect justice from one's Form mistress."

Grace Russell was a decided success as Warden. She was not the cleverest girl in the Upper Fourth by any means, but she was one of the oldest, and she had a strong sense of duty. She kept the rules scrupulously herself, and discouraged all the shirkings that had come in under Hope's regime. It was wonderful how rapidly most of the girls responded to her influence, and how soon the Form began to take a better tone.

Hope was very quiet and subdued after her deposition, till one day she caught Dorothy in the dressing-room.

"You're a mean sneak, Dorothy Greenfield!" she began hotly. "You promised on your honour you wouldn't tell Miss Tempest we'd been at the wedding, and yet you went and did it!"

"I didn't!" declared Dorothy, with equal heat. "I kept my promise absolutely. I never told a single soul."

"What's the quarrel?" said Margaret Parker.

"Why, Dorothy had seen Blanche and me at that wretched wedding—I wish we'd never gone!—and she promised she wouldn't tell, and then she must have done—I'm certain it was she!"

"It was Professor Schenk who told Miss Tempest," replied Margaret. "I know, because Beatrice Schenk said so. Do you mean to say you let Dorothy own up about that business, and then expected her to keep quiet about your share of it? It's you who are the sneak. Dorothy tell, indeed! We know her better than that. She flies into rages, but she'd scorn to get anybody into trouble at head-quarters. I think she's been a trump."

The feeling of the Form at present was decidedly in Dorothy's favour. Schoolgirl opinion veers round quickly, and a companion who is unpopular one week may be a heroine the next. Margaret Parker was so indignant at Hope's conduct that she published abroad the story of the promise, and the general verdict was that Dorothy had shown up very well in the affair.

"I don't believe I'd have kept such a secret and let Hope get off scot-free," said Ruth Harmon, "especially when she was being so rude; but I'm not quixotic, so that makes the difference."

After this the rehearsals in the gymnasium went on briskly. It was growing near Christmas, and there was still much to be done to perfect the performance. Dorothy threw herself with enthusiasm into the part of Becky Sharp; she did it to the life, and defied Miss Pinkerton with special zeal.

"She does it almost too well. I wish Miss Tempest could see her!" laughed Alison.

"She's going to," said Mavie. "She sent a message to say she'd like to come, and bring some of the mistresses."

"Oh! Oh! Oh!" exclaimed the girls.

The little play had only been intended to be acted before a select circle of day boarders, so the performers felt quite nervous at the idea of numbering Miss Tempest and the mistresses among their audience. It was to be given at two o'clock on the last Tuesday before breaking-up day. It was not possible to make many preparations in the way of scenery, but the girls did their best in respect of costumes. Alison coaxed two silk dresses and several other properties from her mother, not to speak of the gorgeous robes in the chest which she brought, though it was decided after all not to have tableaux. Poor Alison, still feeling sore about the invitation she had not been allowed to ratify, was determined to lend Dorothy the best pieces of her theatrical wardrobe, and pressed the handsomest things she possessed upon her. She was amply satisfied with the result when she saw her friend attired, as Becky, in a green silk dress and sandalled slippers.

"You're just like the illustrations to our *Vanity Fair*. That little muslin apron's sweet!" she exclaimed.

When the afternoon arrived, not only Miss Tempest and five mistresses, but several members of the Sixth Form took their places on the benches set ready for them.

"Mary Galloway's come! Aren't you nervous, Dorothy?" whispered Ruth, greatly excited, for Mary was the president of the College Dramatic Union, and a critic of matters theatrical.

Dorothy had got to a stage beyond nervousness. She felt as if she were going to execution.

"I expect I shall spoil the whole thing, but it can't be helped," she replied resignedly. With the first sentences, however, her courage returned, and she "played up" splendidly. Her representation of Becky was so spirited that teachers and elder girls applauded loudly.

"Very good indeed," commented Miss Tempest, when the act was over. "I had no idea you could all do so well."

"I should like a word with Becky Sharp," said Mary Galloway, slipping behind the scenes and drawing that heroine aside. Dorothy returned from the whispered conference with shining eyes.

"What is it? You're looking radiant!" said Alison.

"I may well be! Mary Galloway's going to propose me as a member of the College Dramatic Union!"

CHAPTER X
MARTHA REMEMBERS

For Dorothy the Christmas holidays passed quietly and most uneventfully. She and Aunt Barbara saw little of the outside world. It had certainly cost Dorothy several pangs to hear the girls at the College discussing the many invitations they had received and the dances they expected to attend, and to feel that a visit to the vicarage was all the festivity that would be likely to come her way. There were no parties or pantomimes included in her holiday programme. Aunt Barbara had had many expenses lately, and her narrow income was stretched to its fullest extent to pay school fees and the price of the contract ticket.

"It's hateful to be poor," thought Dorothy. "I want pretty dresses and parties like other girls;" and she went home with the old wrinkle between her brows, and a little droop at the corners of her mouth.

If Aunt Barbara noticed these and divined the cause, she made no comment; she did not remind Dorothy of how much she had given up on her behalf, or of what real sacrifice it entailed to send her to Avondale. She took the opportunity, however, one day to urge her to work her hardest at school.

"You may have to earn your own living some time, child," she said. "If anything happens to me, my small pension goes back to the owner of the Sherbourne estate. I shall be able to leave you nothing. A good education is the only thing I can give you, so you must try to make the most of it."

"Shall I have to be a teacher?" asked Dorothy blankly.

"I don't know. It will depend on what I can have you trained for," replied Miss Sherbourne.

She was hurt sometimes by Dorothy's manner; the girl seemed dissatisfied, though she was evidently making an effort to hide the fact.

"It's hard for her to mix at school with girls who have so many more advantages," thought Aunt Barbara. "Was I wise to send her to Avondale, I wonder? Is it having the effect of making her discontented? It's only lately she's grown like this—she was never so before."

Discontented exactly described Dorothy's state of mind. She considered that Fate had used her unkindly. The prospect of gaining her own living was extremely distasteful to her. She hated the idea of becoming a teacher, and no other work seemed any more congenial.

"I'd always looked forward to enjoying myself when I was grown up," she thought bitterly, "and now it will be nothing but slave."

At present Dorothy was viewing life entirely from her own standpoint, and was suffering from an attack of that peculiar complaint called "self-itis". She was aggrieved that the world had not given her more, and it never struck her to think of what she might give to the world. It seemed as if she could no longer enjoy all the little simple occupations in which she had been accustomed to take so much pleasure—she was tired of her stamps and postcards, bookbinding and clay modelling had lost their attraction, and she was apathetic on the subject of fancy work.

"I don't know what's come over you," declared Martha. "You just idle about the house doing nothing at all. Why can't you take your knitting, or a bit of crochet in your fingers?"

"Simply because I don't want to. I wish you'd leave me alone, Martha!" replied Dorothy irritably.

She resented the old servant's interference, for Martha was less patient and forbearing than Aunt Barbara, and hinted pretty plainly sometimes what she thought of her nursling.

So the holidays passed by—dreary ones for Dorothy, who spent whole listless evenings staring at the fire; and drearier still for Aunt Barbara, who made many efforts to interest the girl, and, failing utterly, went about with a new sadness in her eyes and a fresh grief in her heart that she would not have confessed to anyone.

Everybody at Holly Cottage was glad when the term began again.

"I don't hold with holidays," grumbled Martha. "Give young folks plenty of work, say I, and they're much better than mooning about with naught to do. Dorothy's a different girl when she's got her lessons to keep her busy."

To do Dorothy justice, she certainly worked her hardest at the College, though the prospect of becoming a teacher did not strike her as an inspiring goal for her efforts. She put the idea away from her as much as possible, but every now and then it returned like a bad nightmare.

"I should hate to be Miss Pitman," she remarked one day at school. "It must be odious to be a mistress."

"Do you think so?" replied Grace Russell. "Why, I'd love it! I mean to go in for teaching myself some time."

"But will you have to earn your own living? I thought your father was well off," objected Dorothy.

"That's no reason why I shouldn't be of some use in the world," returned Grace. "Teaching is a splendid profession if one does it thoroughly. I have a cousin who's a class mistress at a big school near London, and she's so happy—her girls just adore her. It must be an immense satisfaction to feel one's doing some real work, and not being a mere drone in the hive."

This was a new notion to Dorothy, and though she could not quite digest it at first, she turned it over in her mind. She was astonished that Grace, who had a beautiful home, could wish to take up work.

"She'd make a far better teacher, though, than Miss Pitman," she thought. "I wonder why? It's something about Grace that makes one feel—well, that she's always doing things from a motive right above herself."

Dorothy found this an interesting term at the College. As a recruit of the Dramatic Union, she attended rehearsals and was given a minor part in a play that the members were acting, just for practice. It was an honour to be included in the "Dramatic", for its numbers were limited, and it was mostly made up of girls from the Upper School. Her bright rendering of her small part won her notice among the monitresses.

"Dorothy Greenfield is decidedly taking," said Mary Galloway. "She's as sharp as a needle. I believe I like her."

"Um—yes—a little too cheeky for my taste," replied Alice Edwards. "What's the matter with her at present is that she thinks the world is limited to Dorothy Greenfield."

"You've hit the mark exactly," returned Mary.

About the end of January Miss Tempest introduced a new feature at the College. This was a Guild of First Aid and Field Ambulance, and, though it was not incorporated with any special organization, it was drawn up somewhat on the same lines as the Girl Guides. The main object was character training, as developed through work for others. Every member of the Guild was pledged to Chivalry, Patriotism, Self-reliance, and Helpfulness; and her aim was to acquire knowledge to make her of service, not only to herself, but to the community. Membership was not obligatory, but the scheme was so well received that more than half the school joined, Dorothy and Alison being among the number.

"I had to coax Mother tremendously," said Alison. "At first she said no. You see, she thought it was something like the Boy Scouts, and she said she couldn't have me careering about the country on Saturday afternoons—she didn't approve of it for girls."

"But we aren't to go out scouting."

"No; I explained that, and then she gave way. She says she's not sure whether she'll let me go to the Field Ambulance meetings, though; she's afraid I'll catch cold. But I didn't argue about that; I was glad enough to persuade her to say yes on any terms."

"You'll have the ambulance work at school."

"Yes, and perhaps I may go to at least one camp, if the weather's fine."

The Avondale Guild of Help, as it was called, though it began primarily with ambulance, took a wide scope for its work.

"I don't want you to think it is only practising bandaging and having picnics in the country," said Miss Tempest, in her first address to the members. "What is needed is the principle of learning to give willing aid to others, and wishing to be of service. In Japan, when a child is born, a paper sign of a doll or a fish is put up outside the house, to signify whether the baby is a girl or a boy—the boy being destined to swim against the stream and make his own way in the world, and the girl being a doll to be played with. This idea does not meet our present-day standards in England. We do not want our girls to grow up dolls, but helpful comrades and worthy citizens of the Empire. It is terrible to me to think of girls, after their schooldays are over, leading aimless, idle, profitless lives, when there is plenty of good work waiting to be done in the world. 'To whom much is committed, of the same shall much be required', and the education you receive here should be a trust to hand on to others who have not had your advantages. There is nobody who cannot make some little corner of the world better by her presence, and be of use to her poorer neighbours, and I hope the Guild may lead to many other schemes. For the present, I want every member to promise to make one garment a year as her contribution to our charity basket. The clothes will be sent to the Ragged School Mission in the town, and distributed to those who badly need them."

Each member of the Guild signed her name on a scroll, pledged herself to observe the rules, and received the badge, a little shield bearing the motto: "As one that serveth".

"I feel almost like a Crusader!" laughed Dorothy, as she pinned on her badge.

"It's a part of the greatest of all crusades," said Grace Russell gravely.

Everybody was delighted with the ambulance classes. They were considered the utmost fun, and the girls looked forward to them from week to week. They were held in the gymnasium, the members practising upon one another. Any stranger suddenly entering the room would have been amazed to see rows of girls lying prostrate on the floor, while amateur nurses knelt by their sides, placing their legs in splints contrived out of hockey sticks, binding up their jaws, or lifting them tenderly and carrying them on improvised stretchers with a swinging "step both together" motion. It was amusing when at a certain signal the nurses and patients changed places; by an apparent miracle the latter kicked away their splints, tore off their bandages, and set to work with enthusiasm to apply treatment to the imaginary injuries of their quondam attendants.

Of course, there were many laughable mistakes. Ruth Harmon got mixed one day in the diagnosis, and insisted upon turning a rebellious patient upon her face.

"What are you doing? You're rolling me over like a log!" protested Joyce. "Do stop!"

"No, I shan't. Let me pull out your tongue. It's to get the water from your mouth," insisted Ruth. "It's no use working your arms when your air passages are choked."

"But I wasn't drowning! I have a broken leg!"

"Then why couldn't you tell me so at first? I thought you were one of those who were supposed to be fished out of the river!"

"I've grown quite clever at pretending fits," said Alison. "I only bargain that they stick my own pocket-handkerchief between my teeth."

"My speciality is a sprained ankle," said Dorothy. "I can hold my foot quite limp and let it waggle."

"It was you who talked when you had a broken jaw, and that's a sheer impossibility," said Annie Gray.

"Well! Who sneezed when we were trying treatment for bleeding from the nose?"

"I couldn't help that; it was a 'physical disability'."

"It's our turn to revive fainting. Who'll do an elegant swoon? Alison, will you?"

"No, thanks. I don't mind fits, but I hate faints. The burnt feather makes me cough, and last time you simply soused me with water. I thought I was being drowned."

As the term went on and the girls became more adept at first aid, Miss Tempest decided to organize a camp drill, and to take them for an afternoon's practice in field work. To Dorothy's delight, a meadow at Hurford was chosen as the scene of action.

"You'll be able to come and watch, Auntie," she said to Aunt Barbara. "We're going to do all sorts of exciting things. We're to suppose there's been a battle, and then we'll come on and help the wounded—carry some of them to transport wagons, and make wind screens for others, and of course bind them all up first. We're to have a lot of little boys from the Orphanage for soldiers—that's why Miss Tempest chose to come to Hurford, because they've a Boy Scout Corps at the Orphanage, and can lend us some real stretchers and a proper ambulance wagon. I hope I shall get a nice bright boy as patient."

After considerable coaxing, Alison managed to persuade her mother to allow her to take part, if the day proved suitable.

"It's so much warmer now, Mother dearest," she pleaded. "I haven't had a cold for ages; and we shan't be standing still—we shall be busy running about all the time. It's only from half-past two till four. You might come and watch."

"It's my afternoon to help at the Sewing Meeting," said Mrs. Clarke. "I could hardly miss that while the Deaconess is away."

"Then drive over to Hurford and fetch me home. I haven't been out in the trap for ages—yes, ages! Do, darling Motherkins! I should so enjoy it, and—oh yes, I'll put a Shetland shawl over my mouth, if you like, and you could bring my thick coat. Will you promise?"

"It depends on the weather, Birdie," replied her mother discreetly.

The afternoon in question turned out mild enough to allay even Mrs. Clarke's fears. It was one of those balmy, delicious days in early spring when the earth seems to throb with renewed life, and there is real warmth in the sunshine. The Guild members had dinner earlier than usual, and caught the two o'clock train to Hurford. The field that had been engaged as their temporary camp was close to the Orphanage, and they found all ready for them on their arrival, from the stretchers to the row of nice little boys in uniform upon whom they were to operate. Everything was strictly business-like. The officers and patrol leaders at once took command, and began to instruct each group of ambulance workers in the particular duties they were expected to perform. One detachment started to build a fire (there is a science in the building of fires in the open), a second ran up the

Red Cross flag and arranged a temporary hospital with supplies from the transport wagon, while a third went out to render first aid to the wounded.

The boys entered thoroughly into the spirit of the affair. A blank charge was fired, at which signal they all dropped down on the grass as "injured".

Dorothy, who was told off to No. 3 Corps, flew at the sound of the guns, and pounced upon the first prostrate form she came across.

"Are you killed or wounded?" she enquired breathlessly.

"Wounded, m'm," replied the boy, with a grin. "But you can't have me, because another lady's got me already. She looks at me and she says: 'Not movable', and she's run to get a spade to dig a 'ole with."

"Oh! To put your hip in, I suppose?"

"Yes, m'm. They don't bury us unless we're killed."

"I should think not!" exclaimed Dorothy, as she hurried away to find a patient who was still unappropriated.

"Anybody attending to you?" she asked a solemn, curly-headed little fellow, who lay under the shade of the hedge with arms stretched in a dramatic attitude on either side of him.

"No, miss—shot through the lungs, and leg shattered," he replied complacently.

"Then it's a case of stop bleeding, bandage, and lift on stretcher. I'll bind you up first, and then call for someone to help to carry you. Can you raise yourself at all on your arm, or are you helpless? Am I hurting you?"

"No, miss—but you do tickle me awful!"

"Never mind; I've almost finished. Now your leg. Which is it—right or left?"

"Left. But lor', if it was really shattered, I'd rather you touched t'other!"

"No, you wouldn't. You'd be grateful to me for saving your life. I'm going to whistle for help. Here comes a corporal. Where's my stretcher sling? Now, Marjorie, let us lift him quickly and gently. That was neatly done! We'll have him in hospital in record time."

Everybody enjoyed the afternoon, the patrols that performed the camp cookery, the first-aid workers, the nursing sisters at the hospital, and the elect few who were initiated into the elements of signalling.

Alison, who had helped to put up a tent, and given imaginary chloroform under the directions of a supposed army surgeon, was immensely proud of herself, and half-inclined to regard the work of the Red Cross Sisterhood as her vocation in life.

"It's ripping!" she declared. "I'd six of the jolliest boys for patients. One of them offered to faint as many times as I liked, and another (he was a cunning little scamp) assured me his case required beef tea immediately it was ready in the camp kitchen. He asked if I'd brought any chocolate. Another was so realistic, he insisted on shrieking every time I touched him, and he groaned till his throat must have ached. I think ambulance is the best fun going."

"We must beseech Miss Tempest to let us have another field day," said Grace Russell, who had been helping with the cookery and carrying round water. "We each want to practise every part of the work so as to be ready for emergencies. It isn't a really easy thing to give a prostrate patient a drink without nearly choking him. One doesn't know all the difficulties until one tries."

"One doesn't, indeed," said Ruth Harmon. "Field work isn't plain sailing. I wish we hadn't to catch the 4.15 train; I should have liked to stay longer. There's the signal to form and march. Aren't you coming, Alison?"

"No; I'm not going by train. My mother promised to drive over for me. I wonder she hasn't arrived."

"Will she come by the high road from Latchworth?" asked Dorothy. "Then walk home with Aunt Barbara and me. We shall very likely meet her on the way."

"Oh, I'd love to see where you live!" exclaimed Alison. "Is that your aunt? She's sweet. I imagined somehow she'd be much older than that. I think she's ever so pretty. I hope Mother'll be late, and that we shall get as far as your house before we meet the trap."

Alison chattered briskly as they walked along the road; she had a very friendly disposition, and was much taken with Miss Sherbourne's appearance. She had not been in Hurford before, so she was interested to notice the fine old church and the picturesque village street.

"It's ever so much prettier than Latchworth," she declared. "I wish our house were here instead. Oh, look at that dear little place with the porch all covered with creepers! Is that yours? How lovely! It looks as if it had stepped out of a picture."

"Won't you come in, dear, and wait for your mother?" said Miss Sherbourne. "We can watch for the trap from the window."

"May I? I'd love to. Oh, Dorothy, while I'm here, do show me your stamps! You always promised to bring them to school, but you never have done it. And I want to look at your clay models too."

"Come to my den, then," said Dorothy. "Martha will stand at the gate and stop the trap from passing, won't you, Martha? Now, Alison, we'll go upstairs."

The two girls had only a very short time in which to examine Dorothy's various possessions. After a few minutes Martha came running up to say that the trap was waiting.

"And the lady said you were please to come at once," she added, addressing Alison.

"Oh, bother," exclaimed the latter; "I haven't seen half yet! I suppose I shall have to go, though. Where's your aunt? I want to say good-bye to her. Oh, there she is at the gate, speaking to Mother!"

Mrs. Clarke was not at all pleased to find her daughter awaiting her at Holly Cottage, though she had the good manners to conceal her feelings and speak politely to Miss Sherbourne; so she hustled Alison into the trap as speedily as possible.

"We're late, Birdie. I couldn't help it—I was delayed at the Sewing Meeting. But we must hurry home now. Here's your shawl, and put this golf cape on. No, child; you must have it properly round you."

"I'm so hot!" panted poor Alison, dutifully submitting to the extra wraps.

"You'll be cold enough driving. Have you tucked the rug thoroughly round your knees? Then say good-bye."

"Good-bye! Good-bye! I hadn't half enough time," cried Alison, trying to wave a hand, in spite of the encumbrance of the golf cape. "I'd like to come again and——" But here her mother whipped up the pony so smartly that the rest of the sentence was lost in the grating of wheels.

"So that is Mrs. Clarke," said Aunt Barbara, as she entered the cottage again. "She looks nice, though I wish she had allowed Alison to stay for a few minutes longer. It's a funny thing, but somehow her face seems so familiar to me. I wonder if I can possibly have met her before?"

"Have you seen her in Coleminster?" suggested Dorothy.

"No; the remembrance seems to be much farther back than that. I should say it was a long time ago."

"So it was—nearly fourteen years," volunteered Martha, who was laying the tea table. "I remembered her fast enough. I knew her the moment I set my eyes on her."

Martha had the privilege of long service, and was accustomed to speak her mind and offer advice to her mistress on many occasions. If she was blunt and abrupt in her manners, she was a very faithful soul, and her north-country brains were shrewd and keen. She was an authority in the little household on many points, and her remarks were never ignored.

"Why, Martha, I always say you've a better memory than I have," returned Miss Sherbourne. "Where did we know her, then?"

"We didn't know her," said Martha, pausing and looking at Dorothy. "The bairn's been told about it now, so I suppose I can speak before her? Well, that lady in the trap to-day is the same one that came to the inn at Greenfield Junction, and was so upset at sight of the child."

"Are you sure, Martha?" exclaimed Miss Barbara.

"Certain; I never forget a face. I'd take my oath before a judge and jury."

"She did not remember us."

"Didn't she? I wouldn't swear to that. You've not changed so much but that anyone would recognize you. It's my opinion she knew us both, and that was the reason she was in such a precious hurry to get away."

CHAPTER XI
ALISON'S UNCLE

Not very long after the events narrated in the last chapter, Alison entered the train one morning in quite a state of excitement, and could scarcely wait to greet Dorothy before she began to pour out her news.

"Mother had a letter yesterday by the afternoon post. It was from Uncle David, and he's actually on his way home to England. He's not going back to India at all; he wants to settle down near Latchworth. He'll get here before Easter, and he's coming straight to stay with us. Isn't it lovely?"

"Are you fond of him?" enquired Dorothy.

"Oh, he's just ripping! He's so jolly, you know, always having jokes and fun with me. He's the only uncle I possess, so of course I make the most of him; but he's as good as a dozen."

"And I don't possess even one," thought Dorothy. "Have you any cousins?" she added aloud.

"Only seconds and thirds once removed. They're so distant, I can scarcely count them as relations. My one first cousin died when she was a baby, and Aunt Madeleine died too—out in India—so poor Uncle David has been alone ever since. But he's always fearfully busy; he goes about superintending railways and building bridges. He has a whole army of coolies under him sometimes, and they have to take the lines through jungles where there are tigers, and snakes, and things. He writes us the most tremendously interesting letters. Oh, I'm just longing to hear all his stories! When I can get him in the right mood and he starts, he yarns on for hours, and it's so fascinating, I never want him to stop."

"So he is to stay at your house?"

"Rather! We'd be fearfully cross with him if he didn't. He's coming to us first, and then he and Mother and I are all going away somewhere for the Easter holidays. It will be such fun! I wish the time would fly quicker."

"It's only a fortnight to the end of the term now," said Dorothy.

"I know, but a fortnight is fourteen days, my dear. Mother says Uncle David will probably arrive at the end of next week, though; she thinks he may come overland from Marseilles. She wants to arrange to go away on the Wednesday before Easter at latest. I don't expect I shall come to school for the last day—perhaps not in the last week at all. Mother can't bear travelling when the trains are crowded, so we may start on the Monday or Tuesday."

"What place are you going to?"

"I don't know. We're leaving that for Uncle David to decide."

It must be delightful, thought Dorothy, to have the anticipation of such a pleasant holiday. Alison was much to be envied, not only for the possession of so desirable an uncle, but because he seemed disposed to spend his time in the company of his niece, and to entertain her with tales of adventure.

"I don't suppose I shall see him," she said to herself. "They won't ask me to Lindenlea; but I should like to hear some of the stories about India. Well, luck never comes my way. Nobody's going to take me away from home this Easter."

Sometimes when we are railing our hardest at Fate, and calling her by opprobrious names, she astonishes us by twisting round her mystic wheel and sending us an unwonted piece of good fortune. Dorothy had often bemoaned the fact that nobody ever asked her away; yet only a week afterwards she received an invitation, and that from a most unexpected quarter. She had always been rather a favourite with Dr. Longton, who had attended her in measles, bronchitis, and the few other ailments in which she had indulged; and also with Mrs. Longton, a kind-hearted, elderly lady, whose daughters were all married and living in Coleminster. On the Saturday before Easter Mrs. Longton called on Miss Sherbourne, mentioned that she and the doctor were going to the Dales for a little holiday, and asked if Dorothy might be allowed to accompany them.

"We had arranged to take my niece," she explained, "but her mother is unwell, and she cannot leave home at present. We had engaged a bedroom for her at the Hydro., so we shall be delighted if Dorothy will occupy it instead. We are both fond of young people, and it will be a pleasure to have her with us. Would you care to come, my dear?"

Dorothy's face was such a beaming advertisement of joy that her instant acquiescence seemed superfluous. Aunt Barbara readily agreed, and in a few minutes the whole plan was discussed and fixed.

"Isn't it too lovely!" cried Dorothy, exulting over her invitation when Mrs. Longton had gone. "I've never in my life stayed at a hydro. And to go to Clevedale, too! I suppose it's splendid. Bertha Warren was at Ringborough last summer, and she raved over it. Auntie, don't you think for once I'm in luck's way? I believe it's because I bought a swastika at the bazaar, and have worn it ever since, though you told me I was silly to spend my sixpence on it."

Aunt Barbara laughed.

"I don't believe in charms. I remember I found a horseshoe on the very day I sprained my ankle, long ago, and the biggest cheque I ever received came immediately after I had spilt a whole salt-cellar full of salt. But I certainly agree that you're a lucky girl. It's extremely kind of the Longtons to take you."

"And we're starting next Thursday! Hip, hip, hooray!" sang Dorothy, hopping into the kitchen to tell Martha her good news.

It was really a very great event for Dorothy to go from home. Every detail of her preparations and packing was interesting to her. It was delightful to be able to take out the new nightdress-case, and the best brush and comb, which had been lying for so long a time in her bottom drawer, waiting for an occasion such as this; to put fresh notepaper in her writing-case, and to replenish the sewing materials in her blue silk "housewife". There were great debates over her clothing, for she was still growing at such express speed that any garments which had been put away were hopelessly short, particularly the white dress that was to do duty for evening wear.

"I believe it has shrunk!" she exclaimed ruefully.

"No; it's you who have shot up so fast. I wish the clothes grew with you! I must try if I can lengthen it."

Miss Sherbourne had clever fingers, and she contrived to make the necessary alterations so skilfully that nobody would have detected them; and Dorothy declared that, far from being spoilt, the dress was improved.

"I've bought you some new hair ribbons, and you can wear your chain of green Venetian beads," said Aunt Barbara. "Where are your Prayer Book and hymn-book? And your stockings? Bring them here with the other things; we'll pack in my bedroom."

The College broke up for the holidays on the Wednesday before Easter. Alison did not appear at school all that week, so Dorothy supposed that the uncle must have arrived, and that they had gone from home.

"Alison doesn't know I'm having a jaunt too," she thought. "We shall be able to compare notes when we meet again."

On the longed-for Thursday Dorothy, feeling very important and grown-up, met Dr. and Mrs. Longton at the station, and found herself "off and away". The trains were crowded and late, but she enjoyed the journey nevertheless. She had seen so little of the world that it was a delight to her to watch the landscape from the carriage windows; and the bustle of the busy station where they changed amused her, however it might distract Dr. Longton, who was anxious about the luggage. Their destination was Ringborough, a beautiful spot in Clevedale much celebrated for its bracing air and its splendid mountain views. The hydropathic establishment where they were to stay was situated on a pine-clad hillside, and its extensive grounds sloped to a turbulent northern river that swirled along, brown with peat from the moors.

Dr. Longton, who was an enthusiastic angler, and had come armed with a variety of fishing tackle, looked at the condition of the water with a critical eye as he passed.

"Well, when I can't fish I can golf," he remarked. "The links here are among the best in the kingdom. Dorothy, do you feel inclined to act caddy?"

"I'd rather carry your baskets of fish," laughed Dorothy.

"You little impudence! Do you mean to hint that my catches will prove such a light weight? Just wait and see. I'll make you earn your salt, young lady. Perhaps you'll be staggering under a creel like a Newhaven fishwife before you return. Here we are at last. Now, I hope they've really kept the rooms I asked for. I stipulated for a south aspect."

The hydropathic, it appeared, was very full, and the doctor, greatly to his dissatisfaction, was not able to have the particular accommodation for which he had written.

"We must put up with what we can get, I suppose," he grunted. "At this season everybody swarms out of town for a breath of mountain air and a try at the trout."

Dorothy, at any rate, was not disposed to grumble at the little bedroom which fell to her share, though it was on the top story. She liked going up and down in the lift, and her window looked directly out on to the woods at the back. There was a delicious smell of pines in the air, and when she leaned out she could catch a glimpse, round the corner, of a piece of brown river. In the highest spirits she unpacked and changed her dress, and Mrs. Longton came to take her downstairs.

The ways of a hydropathic were unknown to Dorothy; it seemed new and strange to her to enter the large public drawing-room, full of people waiting for the dinner gong to sound. She looked round with keen interest at the other visitors. A large party of gentlemen stood near the piano, discussing fishing prospects; some golfers, collected round the fire, were comparing notes and relating experiences; a few of the ladies were busy with fancy work, and some were reading. Standing by the bookcase, turning over the volumes, was a familiar little figure with a round, rosy face.

"By all that's marvellous, it's Alison!" gasped Dorothy.

The recognition between the two girls was a mutual astonishment. Alison rushed to welcome her friend in great excitement.

"Dorothy, is it really you? Oh, how delightful! Mother, Dorothy's actually staying here! Uncle David, this is my very greatest friend! Oh, what a perfectly lovely surprise! When did you come? We've been here since Monday."

Mrs. Clarke greeted Dorothy coldly, but the pleasant-faced, brown-bearded gentleman addressed as Uncle David smiled as he shook hands.

"So this is your school chum, Birdie? Well, it's a piece of luck for you that she's turned up here. There'll be high jinks now, I expect."

"Rather!" declared Alison, with a beaming look. "It's the one thing that will make the holiday complete."

Though Mrs. Clarke might not share her daughter's enthusiasm at the meeting, she found it impossible to prevent the intimacy between the two girls. She made a struggle at first to keep them apart, but Alison had been spoilt too long not to know how to wheedle her mother and get her own way.

"I can't be rude to Dorothy," she pleaded. "It will seem so extraordinary if I mayn't speak to her."

"I don't forbid you to speak to her, only there is no need for you to spend your whole time together. I don't wish you to be on such familiar terms," replied Mrs. Clarke.

"Nonsense, Cecily!" put in Uncle David, interfering on behalf of his niece. "You're quite absurd over Birdie. The poor child must have some young friends; you can't expect her to be content with us middle-aged people. I like this Dorothy What's-her-name. She has a bright, taking little face. It can't possibly do Birdie any harm to associate with her. You can't bring up the girl in cotton wool. You coddle her enough on the subject of health, so at least let her enjoy herself in other ways. I'm going fishing to-morrow with Dr. Longton—he's a bluff old Yorkshireman, but he's capital company, and he's a member of the North Riding Anglers' Club. He's promised to give me some hints."

With her uncle's influence on her side, Alison felt an official seal had been placed on her friendship; and as Mrs. Longton was pleased for Dorothy to have found a companion, the two girls were much together. Ringborough Hydropathic was a favourite resort for Coleminster people, and two other girls from the College happened to be staying there with their families— Hope Lawson and Gabrielle Helm, who was in the Lower Fifth. Hope did not look particularly pleased to meet her classmates; she gave them each a cool little nod, and took no further notice of them. She was much occupied with her own set of friends, and did not seem disposed to trouble herself with her schoolfellows; nor were they anxious to push themselves under her notice. Gabrielle Helm, on the contrary, claimed acquaintance with Dorothy and Alison, and introduced her brothers, Percy and Eric, who attended the Coleminster Boys' College. The young people were keen on golf, and from them Dorothy received her first lessons on the links, laughing very much over her mistakes and false strokes, and enjoying every moment of the time. She had never spent such holidays, or dreamed that they were even possible; and the days did not seem half or a quarter long enough for all the delightful things there were to do in them.

"It was good of you to bring me," she said sometimes to Mrs. Longton.

"It's a pleasure to see your bright face, my dear," replied her kind chaperon. "You're so rosy, your aunt will hardly know you when you return."

"Dorothy is growing quite pretty," said Gabrielle Helm to Alison. "I used to think her rather a scrawny-looking girl, but she's suddenly developed into almost a beauty. Percy said last night he thought her ripping, and he's a fearful old 'hard-to-please'."

"Yes," said Alison contemplatively, "Dorothy has changed. Of course, her eyes were always lovely, but her face has filled out lately, and she does her hair more becomingly. That's made a difference. And that blue dress suits her. I think she's prettier now than Hope Lawson."

"Hope wouldn't allow that."

"Rather not!" laughed Alison.

Dorothy was indeed having "the time of her life", and very great happiness is often an aid to good looks. Though she found Mrs. Clarke rather chilly and distant, she liked Alison's Uncle David immensely. Sometimes the two girls would accompany him and the doctor on a fishing expedition, or a walk through the pine woods, where he proved the pleasantest and most humorous of companions; or, better still, they would catch him in the half-hour before dinner, decoy him into one of the small sitting-rooms generally empty at that time in the evening, and then cajole him into telling some of his experiences in the jungle. To Dorothy these Indian stories were thrilling; she was never tired of hearing about tigers and elephants, ruined temples, fakirs, coolies, and midnight adventures.

"Of course, Uncle David draws the long bow considerably," laughed Alison. "He expects one to take ten per cent discount off all his traveller's yarns. But they're very fascinating, even if they're not true! He likes you, because you're a good listener. Dorothy, what shall we do without you when the holiday's over?"

"Don't speak of it! I'm living in the present from hour to hour," declared Dorothy.

CHAPTER XII
THE SUBTERRANEAN CAVERN

The Ringborough Hydropathic was not only celebrated for fishing and golf—the neighbourhood itself held many attractions. The mountains round, grim stony ridges, contained curiosities of nature such as are only found in a limestone district. There were wonderful subterranean caverns, full of stalactites and stalagmites; underground lakes and rivers, and mysterious "potholes" leading no one knew whither.

"We ought to make an excursion to Lingham Cave," said Percy Helm one day. "It's one of the local sights, and it seems a pity to miss it. Couldn't we arrange to go altogether in a big party? To-morrow would be a good opportunity."

When to-morrow came, none of the elders seemed disposed to fall in with Percy's plans. Dr. Longton and Mr. Clarke were bent on fishing, Mrs. Longton was tired and preferred to stay in the garden, and Mr. and Mrs. Helm wished to play golf. Mrs. Clarke would not hear of Alison's going on such an expedition.

"I've been before to Lingham," she said, "and I know from experience how damp and cold it is inside the cave. You were coughing last night, Birdie, and I don't want to risk your catching a bad cold. You must be content to do something quiet to-day."

Dorothy easily obtained Mrs. Longton's consent, so she and the three young Helms took packets of lunch and started to walk over the fells to Lingham, a distance of about four miles. The weather was still cold, and the crests of some of the highest hills were tipped with snow. The keen, bracing air felt like a tonic. The four strode along briskly over the short moorland grass, admiring the rugged gorge whence the river flowed first between two sheer walls of limestone, and then through a chasm that seemed to have been made by the rending asunder of a mountain of rock.

"It's a primeval kind of place," said Gabrielle. "One can understand what a terrible upheaval there must have been to split the cliffs and twist all the strata out of shape. What enormous force it must have needed! One wonders if any human beings were there when it happened."

"If there were, they wouldn't be there long," said Percy. "The smallest of those rocks would be enough to crush an army."

"It's a pity Alison isn't here," remarked Dorothy. "She's rather keen on geology, and one gets a much better general view of the gorge from here than from the Hydro."

"Yes, I'm sorry she wasn't allowed to come," replied Gabrielle. "I think Mrs. Clarke is fearfully nervous. I'm glad Mother doesn't fuss over me to such an extent. Still, it has another side to it—it must be rather nice to be a treasured only child!"

"Then you should have been born in a different family; you made a bad choice in ours," said Eric.

"How many of you are there altogether?" asked Dorothy.

"Seven; we've left the little ones behind."

"Only Norma goes to the Coll."

"Yes; the other three are nursery children. You don't know what it is to be eldest daughter. Be thankful you haven't three small nuisances at home."

"I wish I had!" said Dorothy.

"All right; you may change places with me. I'll hand over the whole set of brothers and sisters, Percy and Eric included."

"A happy exchange for us!" murmured Percy, with a look at Dorothy.

"You horrid boy!" said Gabrielle.

"I want to know why Percy has brought that coil of rope with him," enquired Dorothy. "I've been wondering ever since we started."

"Well, I'm quite prepared to satisfy your curiosity. Let us sit down and eat our lunch while I expound; there are some jolly stones here for seats."

All four were very ready for lunch, though it was only twelve o'clock. The keen air had given them fine appetites, and the ham sandwiches and chicken drumsticks disappeared quickly, not to speak of the bread and cheese and cakes.

"They don't put up bad lunches at the Hydro.," said Percy, aiming his last chicken bone at a bird that flew overhead.

"What about the rope?" asked Dorothy again. "I'm still inquisitive."

"It's an idea of mine. You know, everybody goes to Lingham Cave; it's a regular show place. You pay your shilling, and you're taken round by a guide who tells you where to step, and not to knock your head, and all that kind of stuff, and prates away about geology and natural curiosities and the rest of it, as if he'd learnt it off like a lesson. Well, instead of going where everybody else goes, I think it would be much better fun to explore a place of our own. There's another cave at the other side of Lingham, on the spur of Whernscar. I saw the entrance to it last Friday, when I walked over with Dr. Shaw. He pointed it out to me, and said very few people had been down it, but it was quite as fine as the other, and had splendid—what do you call those thingumgigs?—oh yes, stalactites, and an underground waterfall."

A LESSON IN GOLF

"Is there a guide there?" asked Eric.

"No; that's the best of it—no shillings to pay, and no bothering lecture. People fight shy of it because it's so out of the way and rather difficult to go down—the passage is narrow, and there's one bad place. I thought if we had a rope, though, we could manage it easily; and look! I've brought all these candles and three boxes of matches."

"It would be ripping to see an underground waterfall," said Eric. "There isn't one in Lingham Cave."

"Yes; we might never get such an opportunity again. Who votes for Whernscar?"

"I do," said Dorothy promptly. The idea of an adventure tempted her. She was always attracted by the unknown.

"I suppose we should be all right? It will be quite safe, I mean?" queried Gabrielle, a little doubtfully.

"Right as a trivet, with a rope and candles," replied Percy. "I expect if this cave were nearer Lingham village it would be more popular than the other. It's fearfully far from the station, though, which doesn't suit trippers."

"We're trippers ourselves if we make a trial trip," laughed Eric.

All the four young people were excited at the prospect of exploring a little-known cavern without the assistance of a guide. They felt like a band of pioneers in a fresh country, or the discoverers of a new continent. None of them in the least realized the risk of the proceeding, and no older person was there to preach wisdom. Percy, who had been over the fells before, knew the way, and therefore assumed the direction of the party. Instead of going down to Lingham, they turned up the hill instead, and struck across the spur of Whernscar. It was a grim, desolate part of the country; the bare rocks, upheaved in strange shapes and unclothed by any greenery, seemed like the skeleton of the earth exposed to view. Stone walls took the place of hedges, and there was scarcely a human habitation within sight. Scattered here and there over the moorland were curious natural pits called "potholes", deep and dark as wells, and with a sound of rushing water at the bottom. Into one of these a small stream emptied itself, and was swallowed up bodily.

"They're fearful places," said Dorothy, holding Gabrielle's hand, and gazing half-fascinated over the edge of the pit into the bubbling depths below. "It's like a witch's cauldron; you feel there's 'double, double, toil and trouble' going on down there."

"People must have been fearfully superstitious about these holes in olden times," remarked Gabrielle.

"Rather! They attributed them to His Satanic Majesty—thought they were the blowholes of the nether world, in fact. I don't suppose any of the natives here would care to go near them at night," said Percy.

"Come along! It makes me dizzy to stare down," said Gabrielle. "I feel as if something were drawing me in."

"The wizard who lives at the bottom!" laughed Dorothy. "We're certainly in a very peculiar part of the country. Is it far to the cave now?"

"No, we're quite close. I have my bearings, and I'm pretty sure that it's just round the other side of that crag."

"How exciting! Do let us be quick!"

The mouth of the cave proved to be a small, narrow opening in the side of the hill, no taller or wider than the little postern gate of an old castle. For a few yards inside there was a brown glimmer, but beyond lay inky darkness. The girls, after a first peep, drew back with a shudder, half of real fear, and half of delighted anticipation of a new experience. Percy had taken out the candles and was busy lighting them.

"There's one for each of us," he said. "And we must each have some matches in our pockets, in case of emergencies."

"What emergencies?" asked Gabrielle.

"Well, suppose we got separated?"

"Separated! Don't talk of it. You're not going to lose me, I can tell you. I shall hold on to your coat the whole way. I shan't go in at all if you mean to play hide-and-seek. Promise you won't lose me!"

"Don't be silly! Nobody wants to lose you," said Percy. "I'm only taking proper precautions. There! Are you ready? Eric and I will go first, and you and Dorothy can follow."

"Shades of Pluto, it's spooky!" exclaimed Eric, leading the way.

The passage ran level for about fifteen yards, then began abruptly to descend into the hollow of the mountain. The walls were jagged and uneven, there were frequent turnings and windings, and the floor was rough with small stones or lumps of rock. In two or three places it was very damp. Moisture dripped from the roof and oozed in limestone tears down the walls, forming slimy, milky pools under foot. In the distance they could hear the gurgling of water. The two boys, as pioneers, walked slowly, holding their lights so as to examine well the ground in front. The girls followed them closely.

"I should think it's like this in the Catacombs," said Gabrielle.

"It reminds me of the story of the Princess and the Goblin," said Dorothy.

"Haven't read it."

"You benighted girl! What you've missed! It's the most gorgeous tale that was ever written. The goblins lived in a mountain just like this; they had a great underground hall, and dwellings in mysterious corners and caves. They wanted to steal the little Princess Irene, to marry her to their Prince, only Curdie outwitted them. I feel as if we're following Irene's thread at present."

"I hope you're following me," said Eric. "We're coming to a bad place, so you'd better go carefully."

The floor of the passage, which had been growing more and more uneven and rugged, suddenly shelved down like a ladder.

"Yes, this is a bad bit," muttered Percy. "It will certainly need care. What a good thing I brought the rope!"

"Are you sure it's safe to venture?" asked Gabrielle.

"Yes; it's difficult, but it's safe enough. Dr. Shaw told me about this place. It's called 'The Chute'; it's something like a long smooth slide. We must lower one another with the rope."

"Who is to lower the last?" said Dorothy.

"Oh, I'll manage to climb down all right without. Eric can go first, then he can help you two girls at the bottom."

Eric, with the rope tied round his waist, and his candle held well overhead, started cautiously down the incline in a sitting posture.

"It's as smooth as a slide," he called. "Don't pay out the rope too fast, old chap. Let me down gently. That's better. I'm getting along famously now. I can steady myself with one hand on the wall. Whew! That was a scorcher! There's a nasty twist here. Steady! Let go a bit! Right-o! Here I am!"

The tension on the rope stopped, so he had evidently reached his goal. The others, peering into the darkness, could just see the glimmer of his candle round a piece of projecting rock.

"Where are you?" they shouted.

"In a much wider passage. Come on! I've untied the rope, so you can wind it up. It isn't really difficult at all going down, if you're careful of this corner at the end. I'll climb up and give you each a hand as you come round."

"You go next, Dorothy," said Gabrielle.

It was rather a horrible experience, Dorothy thought, after the rope was tied round her waist, to start on that steep, dark descent, even though Eric was waiting to help her at the bottom. The chute was moist, and as slippery as ice; she felt dreadfully helpless, and if it had not been for the staying power of the rope, she would have shot down as if she had been tobogganing. She managed to aid herself a little by grasping angles of the wall, though one hand was incommoded by holding the candle.

"It's all right. Don't squeak—you've got over the worst now," said Eric, extending a welcome grip at the awkward corner. "Put your foot against that ledge; now then, swing yourself round.—Hi! More rope, up there!—Let yourself slide now—it's only a few feet. You've done it! Hooray!"

Dorothy felt like a heroine as she scrambled to her feet and untied the rope. She peeped anxiously up the chute to see how Gabrielle would fare. The latter, after protesting vigorously that she daren't and couldn't and wouldn't, was at length persuaded to try, and accomplished the descent with many squeals of terror.

"Pooh! What a fuss you girls make!" said Eric. "There's nothing to be frightened about."

When his sister was safely landed at the bottom, Percy managed to descend unaided, and the four started once more on their march of exploration. They were now in a long gallery, much loftier and wider than the passage above. It extended for about a hundred feet, then narrowed and lowered abruptly, so that for a few yards they were obliged to stoop to get along. Suddenly they all stopped with a cry of amazement: the passage ended with a natural arch, and they found themselves staring into a vast subterranean chamber. The cavern was oval in shape, and had probably once been an underground reservoir for water. From the roof, like huge icicles, hung innumerable stalactites, many of which, meeting with stalagmites that rose from the floor, formed pillars as beautiful as the marble columns in a Greek temple. In the faint light of the four candles the scene was immensely impressive. The cave seemed to stretch before the spectators like the dim aisles of some great cathedral. They could not see to its farthest extent, but from somewhere in the distance came the noise of rushing water. Walking carefully between the stalagmites, they commenced a tour of investigation, holding the lights high above their heads, so as to gain as good a view as possible.

"If we only had a piece of magnesium ribbon to burn, wouldn't it be magnificent?" sighed Percy.

"Or even a motor lamp," added Eric.

Guided by the sound of the water, they reached the corner of the chamber, where a natural wonder presented itself. From a hole about fifteen feet above them issued a cascade, which poured in a foaming fall over a ledge of rock, ran for a distance of about eight yards over the floor of the cavern, then plunged into a deep hole and disappeared.

"I wonder where it comes out—if it ever comes out at all?" said Dorothy, shuddering as she watched the black water whirl into the dark abyss.

"Lower down the mountain, probably, but I shouldn't care to try the experiment of jumping in to find out," said Eric. "It's a weird place, but it's worth seeing. I'm glad we came. I believe it's finer than Lingham. And we've done it on our own, too, without any bothersome guide."

"We've got to go back yet," said Gabrielle. "Hadn't we better make a start? It must be getting late."

"Exactly twenty minutes to four," said Percy, consulting his watch.

"Then we must go at once. Remember, we have a long walk before us."

Quite loath to leave the marvels of the subterranean chamber, they tore themselves away, each first breaking off a small stalactite as a souvenir.

"I shall treasure my limestone 'icicle'," said Dorothy. "I shall score if I take it to the geology class at school."

"I've got an extra one to give to the College museum," said Gabrielle. "I hope they won't break in my pocket. I've wrapped them carefully in my handkerchief."

Arrived at the chute, Percy climbed up first, with one end of the rope in his hand, then, stationing himself firmly at the top, announced his readiness to haul up the others. Gabrielle started next, crawling on hands and knees, and helping herself as best she could by the projections of rock at the side. It was much more difficult to ascend than to descend, for the surface was so smooth and slippery, it was impossible to get any grip. Almost her whole weight depended upon the rope; she was a heavy girl, and the strain was great. Percy at the top heaved with all his strength.

"Oh dear, it's dreadful!" cried Gabrielle. "It's cutting my waist in two. Wait a moment, Percy; don't tug so hard. I want to catch this ledge."

"Let go of the rock, and I'll give one good pull," commanded Percy. "If you'll trust yourself absolutely to me, I'll have you up in a jiffy."

Gabrielle loosened her hold, and for one moment threw herself entirely upon the rope. Perhaps it was not strong enough for the purpose, or possibly it had been frayed in the descent by contact with a sharp rock; there was a snap, a sudden, agonized cry, and Gabrielle was precipitated to the bottom of the chasm. She fell heavily, extinguishing her candle as she went, and rolling almost to the feet of Eric and Dorothy, who were standing at the bottom of the chute looking upwards.

"Good gracious! What's happened? Gabrielle, are you hurt?" ejaculated Percy, descending to the rescue with more haste than discretion, and bending over the prostrate form of his sister. "Hold a light, Eric; I can't see her face."

"Oh! Oh! I thought I was being killed!" gasped Gabrielle, raising herself to a sitting position. "Give me your hand, Percy. Oh! Stop, stop! My foot! I believe I've broken my ankle!"

The explorers stared at one another in blankest dismay. This was indeed a predicament. What were they to do, buried in the depths of the earth, and miles away from help of any kind?

"Are you sure it's broken, or could you manage to get up if we each took your arm?" suggested Eric.

"No! No! Don't touch me! It's agony if I move."

"Better let me pull your boot off, quick!" said Dorothy, dropping on her knees by the side of her friend.

It was a very different matter applying First Aid here from what it had been at the ambulance class in the gymnasium at the College. Except pocket-handkerchiefs, there were no materials of any kind to be had. Splints were an impossibility. Dorothy bound up the foot as well as she could, but her every touch was painful to her poor patient.

"You're sitting in such a wet place! Couldn't we lift you just a little?" she suggested.

"No; please leave me alone. Never mind the wet."

Gabrielle's rosy cheeks had grown very white. She looked almost ready to faint. The two boys turned to each other in desperation.

"We can't haul her up that chute with a broken ankle," said Percy. "I must go back to the Hydro. for help, and you must stay with her. I'll be as quick as I possibly can—I'll run all the way."

"Mind you don't tumble into any 'potholes', then," called Gabrielle anxiously, as he scrambled up the chasm and departed.

Then began a long, weary vigil of many interminable hours. The candles had burnt so low that the trio did not dare to have them all lighted together, in case they should be left in the dark before assistance came. They therefore used one at a time, and by its faint gleam the deep shadows of the rocks appeared more dim and gloomy than ever.

"It's almost like being buried alive!" shivered Gabrielle.

"I'm glad Alison didn't come with us," said Dorothy.

"We've landed ourselves in an uncommonly tight fix," remarked Eric.

Would the time never pass? Hour after hour went by. Wet, cold, and hungry, and chilled to the bone, the unfortunate trio sat and waited. They were almost in despair when at last they heard a distant shout, and a few moments afterwards a strong light flashed down the chasm. The band of rescuers proved to consist of Mr. Helm, Dr. Shaw (the medical attendant of the Hydropathic), Dr. Longton, Mr. Clarke, and two gardeners who were well acquainted with the neighbourhood, Percy, of course, leading the way. They had brought motor lanterns, ropes, and a number of other appliances, the most important of all in the eyes of the three shivering young people being a Thermos flask full of hot soup.

The first duty for the doctors was to set the broken ankle; then came the more critical task of removing the injured girl from the cave. Her father, who was fortunately the tallest and strongest member of the party, took her in his arms, and, aided partly by ropes and partly by the help of Dr. Longton and Mr. Clarke, he succeeded in carrying her up the slippery chute on to the level above. Even there their troubles were not over—the many twistings and windings and angles of the tortuous passage were difficult to negotiate without giving undue pain to poor Gabrielle, who was already suffering enough. Her rescuers were only able to proceed very slowly, and with frequent intervals of rest, and by the time the party reached the surface of the fell it was past eleven o'clock.

None of them ever forgot that weird midnight walk back to Ringborough. It was a wild, windy night, with heavy clouds chasing one another across the sky and obscuring the light of the waning moon. Hirst and Chorley, the two gardeners, led the way with the lanterns; then came Mr. Helm and Dr. Shaw, carrying Gabrielle on an improvised stretcher; and the others followed closely behind, Dr. Longton helping Dorothy. The ground was rough and stony, and every now and then their guides had to stop to take their bearings, for there were several "potholes" and other danger spots to be avoided. The first grey streak of dawn was showing in the sky when the party, thoroughly exhausted, at last arrived at the Hydropathic.

"Gabrielle won't be at the Coll. again for ever so long," said Alison to Dorothy next day. "Dr. Shaw thinks it may be six weeks before she's able to walk. Uncle David says it's a miracle she wasn't killed. I'm glad I didn't go—and yet" (rather wistfully) "I don't suppose I shall ever have the opportunity of a real adventure again. It must have been so exciting!"

"It's nicer to read about adventures than to have them," said Dorothy. "It wasn't thrilling at all at the time—it was cold and wet and horrid. I'm delighted to have seen the cave, but I wouldn't go through last night again—not if anyone offered me a hundred pounds!"

CHAPTER XIII
A SCHOOL ANNIVERSARY

Dorothy returned to Hurford with a whole world of new experiences to relate to Aunt Barbara. The visit to Ringborough had indeed been an immense enjoyment, and after so much excitement it was difficult to settle down to the round of school and lessons. With some natures change is a tonic that sets them once more in tune with their everyday surroundings; but with others it only rouses desires for what they cannot get. Unfortunately it had this effect in Dorothy's case. Her pleasant time at the Hydropathic, the amusements there, and her companionship with other young people, which she had so much appreciated, all combined to bring out into sharp contrast the quietness and uneventfulness of her ordinary existence, and to make her life at Holly Cottage seem dull and monotonous. The old cloud settled down upon her, and the old discontented look crept back into her eyes.

Aunt Barbara, who had hoped the holiday would cheer her up, was frankly disappointed. She was uneasy and anxious about Dorothy; she felt that some undesirable element was working in the girl's mind, yet she could not define exactly of what it consisted. It was a negative rather than a positive quality, and manifested itself more in acts of omission than those of commission. Dorothy was rarely disagreeable at home, but she had lately slidden out of many of the little pettings and fond, loving ways that had meant so much to Aunt Barbara, and her manner had grown somewhat hard and uncompromising. Small things count for so much in daily life, and Dorothy, absorbed in her own troubles, never thought what value might be set on a kiss, or what the lack of it might seem to that tender heart which had made her happiness its own.

At present she was engrossed in Avondale concerns, for the coming term was the fullest and busiest in the school year. Not only was there the work of her own form to be considered, but the many side interests in connection with the College also—the Ambulance Guild, the Botanical Society (a special feature of the summer months), and last, but not least, the Dramatic Union, to be a member of which she was justly proud. Her inclusion in this, though a supreme satisfaction, brought the penalty of added work. She was expected to learn parts and submit to severe drilling at rehearsals, the standard required being greatly above what had contented the Upper Fourth.

The Union was looking forward to shortly displaying its talent on the occasion of the school festival. This was to be held on the twelfth of May, partly because it was the anniversary of the laying of the foundation stone of the present building, and partly because, being old May Day, it gave an opportunity for many quaint and charming methods of celebration.

Miss Tempest, who loved to revive bygone customs, had introduced maypole plaiting, morris dances, and other ancient "joyous devices" at the school, and the girls had taken them up with enthusiasm. At this festival, instead of giving dances and May Day carols, such as had been popular for the last year or two, the Dramatic Union was to act a floral pageant called "The Masque of the Blossoms", a pretty performance in which interesting old catches and madrigals were included, and many historical and emblematical characters represented. Miss Hicks, the singing mistress, undertook the direction of the musical part of the piece, and coached the girls at private practices in the songs.

Dorothy, after the allotment of the parts, came home brimming over with excitement.

"It's the most delightful, quaint thing, Auntie! 'Queen Elizabeth' is in it, and 'Raleigh' and 'Spenser', as well as 'Venus' and two nymphs, and the spirit of the woodlands. The songs are charming. I know you'll like 'Now is the month of maying' and 'The trees all budding'. Nora Burgess is to be 'Leader of the Masque', and Ottilia Partington is 'Spring'. And oh, Auntie! what do you guess is my part? I'm to be 'Queen of the Daffodils'! It lay between me and Vera Norland; we both knew the words equally well, so we drew lots, and I won. I've brought a book to show you what the costume must be. Look! it gives a picture."

"It's extremely pretty, but it seems rather elaborate," said Miss Sherbourne, scanning the dainty creation figured in the illustration with an eye to its home-dressmaking possibilities.

"Do you think so? The green part's to be made of satin, and the skirt underneath is all folds of soft yellow silk, to represent petals. Then there are wreaths of artificial daffodils, and a veil of gauze covered with gold sequins."

"Perhaps we can copy it in sateen and art muslin," said Aunt Barbara.

"Auntie! It ought to be real silk and satin! It won't look anything if it's only made of cheap materials."

"But I can't afford to buy dearer ones for a costume that will only be used once."

"Muriel, and Fanny, and Olga, who are taking the other flowers, are having beautiful things made at a dressmaker's," returned Dorothy rather sulkily.

"I dare say; but that doesn't make it any easier for us."

"I can't be the only one in a cheap dress!" burst out Dorothy. "Oh, Auntie, you might let me have something nice, just for once! It's too bad that I never get anything like other girls."

"You don't know what you ask, Dorothy," said Miss Sherbourne, with a pained tone in her voice. "I do all for you that's in my power. It hurts me to deny you even more than it hurts you to go without what you want. No, I can't promise anything; you must learn to realize what a small margin we have for luxuries."

Dorothy flung down the book and rushed upstairs to her bedroom. She was thoroughly out of temper, and hot tears started to her eyes. She had set her heart on making a good effect as "Queen of the Daffodils". It was an important part in the Masque, and she was extremely triumphant that the lot had fallen to her. To act at the College Anniversary was a great honour, and Dorothy knew that Hope Lawson and Valentine Barnett, neither of whom was included this time, would have been only too delighted to have her chance.

"They envy me ever so much, and it will make them extra-censorious," she thought. "They'll turn up their noses dreadfully if I only wear a costume of sateen and art muslin."

To Dorothy, who had not yet forgotten her disappointment at losing the election for the Wardenship, and who was always on the defensive against real or imaginary slights, this occasion of the festival seemed a unique opportunity of asserting her position in the school. She knew, from former experience, how the girls discussed and criticized the dresses worn by the players, and what elaborate and expensive costumes were often provided: many beautiful accessories in the way of scenery were generally lent by parents of the pupils, and the whole performance was on a very handsome scale. To be one of the masquers in this year's pageant would increase her social standing, and magnify her importance in her Form as nothing else could possibly do. She pictured the triumph of the scene, the select company of picked actors on the platform, the music, the flowers, and the lovely effects of colour grouping. The large lecture hall would be filled to overflowing with pupils and guests. Alison's uncle would no doubt be there, and Percy and Eric Helm. She would like them to see her as "Queen of the Daffodils". She might give three "performer's invitations", so she could ask Dr. and Mrs. Longton as well as Aunt Barbara. Oh, it would be the event of her life! But how was all this to happen if she could not be provided with a suitable costume?

"What it comes to is this," she said to herself. "The thing, to be done at all, ought to be done well; the girls will laugh at me if I turn up in sateen, with sixpence-halfpenny bunches of daffodils. I'd rather not act if I can't have a nice dress. Aunt Barbara might manage it somehow."

Dorothy did her lessons in her den that evening, although there was no fire and the weather was still cold. She came down to supper so moody and unresponsive that Miss Sherbourne, after a vain attempt at conversation, gave up the effort, and the meal passed almost in silence. The subject of the Masque was not mentioned by either.

Dorothy cried bitterly in bed that night, hot scalding tears of disappointment—tears that did not soften and relieve her grief, but only made it harder to bear; and she woke next morning with a splitting headache.

"Have you finished with this book, Auntie?" she said after breakfast, taking up the ill-fated catalogue of costumes, which had been left the night before on the sideboard.

"You might leave it for a day or two, if Miss Hicks can spare it," replied Miss Sherbourne. "There is still plenty of time before May the twelfth."

"What's the matter with Dorothy?" said Mavie Morris that morning at school. "She's so glum and cross, one can't get a civil word from her. When I mentioned the pageant, she nearly snapped my head off."

"Tantrums again, I suppose," said Ruth Harmon, shrugging her shoulders. "The best plan is to leave her alone till she comes out of them. You ought to know Dorothy Greenfield by this time."

"You shouldn't tease her," said Grace Russell.

"I didn't. I only asked her what her dress was to be like, and she told me to mind my own business. All those who are acting are just full of their costumes. They talk of nothing else."

"Is Dorothy's going to be a nice one?" asked Ruth.

"I don't know; she wouldn't tell me anything. Dorothy doesn't generally have handsome things, does she?"

"No; she's one of the plainest-dressed girls in the Form."

"But she'll surely come out in something decent for the Masque! She must, you know."

"Perhaps that's the rub—poor Dorothy!" murmured Grace Russell.

When Dorothy returned home that afternoon she found Miss Sherbourne busy at her writing table. Generally all papers were cleared away before tea-time, and Aunt Barbara was ready to help with lessons, or play games and chat afterwards; to-day, however, she instituted a new regime.

"I am going to write in the evenings now," she said, "so you must be quiet, dear, and not disturb me. I have a piece of work that I particularly want to finish."

Dorothy prepared her German translation and learned her Latin vocabularies, then, taking up a volume of Scott, began to read. It was rather dull with only the scratching of Aunt Barbara's pen to break the silence. She missed their usual game of chess and their pleasant talk. It seemed so extraordinary not to be allowed to say a single word. The next evening and the next the programme was the same. Except at meal times, Dorothy hardly had the opportunity of exchanging ideas with Aunt Barbara. She did not like the innovation.

"Auntie does nothing but write—write—write the whole time," she complained to Martha.

"Yes; she's overdoing it entirely, and I've told her so!" returned Martha indignantly. "She's at it from morning till night, and then she's not finished, for she's sitting up to the small hours. There's no sense in fagging like that. You can't burn a candle at both ends."

"Then why does she?" questioned Dorothy.

"That's what I asked her. She's not strong enough to stand it. She's been ill again lately, and if she doesn't mind she'll have a breakdown."

"Auntie, won't you go to bed early too?" suggested Dorothy, as she said good night, looking rather anxiously at the pale face bent over the papers. Miss Sherbourne put her hand to her head wearily.

"I can't. I must make a push and put in a certain number of hours' work, or these articles will never be finished in time. If I can send them in by the second, and they are accepted, I may possibly get a cheque for them at once. That would just give us time before the twelfth. We can't buy silks and satins without the wherewithal, can we?"

"Oh, Auntie! are you slaving like this for me?" exclaimed Dorothy. "Can't we get the dress any other way?"

"No, dear; I can't afford it out of the house-keeping money, and it is one of my rules never to run into debt for anything. Don't worry; another day will see me through, and I think the editor of the *Coleminster Gazette* will like the articles—they're better than the ones he accepted last year."

Dorothy went upstairs uneasy and dissatisfied with herself. Aunt Barbara's good-night kiss had roused something that had been slumbering for a long time. Thoughts that the girl had suppressed lately began to make themselves heard, and to clamour loudly and reproachfully. She tried to put them away, but they refused to be dismissed. With her eyes shut tight in bed, she seemed to see a vision of Aunt Barbara's tired face as she sat working, working so painfully hard in the sitting-room below.

"And for me—always for me—never for herself," reflected Dorothy. "She hasn't bought a new dress of her own this spring, though she needs one badly."

She looked with compunction next morning at Miss Sherbourne's pale cheeks.

"Does your head ache, Auntie?"

"Yes. I haven't been quite well lately, but I expect it will pass. You shall buy me some phenacetin powders in town; they always do my head good. Dr. Longton recommended them."

"She looks more fit to be in bed than at her writing table," thought Dorothy, as she left the room, armed with the necessary prescription. She hurried away from school at four o'clock in order to give herself time to call at the chemist's, and ran anxiously into the house on her return, bearing the packet of powders in triumph.

"Sh! Sh! Don't make a noise," said Martha, coming from the kitchen. "Your aunt's lying down. I told her it would come to this, and I've proved my words. It's an attack of her old complaint. It always comes back with overwork."

"Is she really very ill?" faltered Dorothy.

"I don't know. I've just sent Jones's boy with a message for Dr. Longton. No, you mustn't go disturbing her till he's been. Take your things off, and I'll bring you your tea."

Dorothy ate her solitary meal in sad distress. She could remember two former illnesses of Aunt Barbara's, and she was old enough now to realize how much cause there was for alarm. She waylaid the doctor on his arrival, and begged him to allow her to be of help.

"If Auntie is really going to be ill like she was before, let me be her nurse," she implored. "I learnt a great deal at the ambulance classes, and I'd carry out every single thing you told me."

"We'll see. I must examine my patient first," replied her old friend.

Dorothy sat on the stairs waiting with a beating heart while Dr. Longton was in Miss Sherbourne's room. She sprang up eagerly as he came out, and accompanied him to the porch. She hardly dared to ask for his verdict.

"Yes, it's a nasty return of the old trouble," said the doctor. "I'm afraid she's in for a sharp attack, but luckily I was sent for in good time, and may be able to stave things off a little. So you're anxious to try your hand at nursing, young woman? Well, I don't see why you shouldn't. You and Martha can manage quite well between you, if you'll only carry out my directions absolutely to the letter. When I suggested sending for a trained nurse, your aunt was very much against the idea—begged me not to, in fact. Martha has a head on her shoulders, and you're not a child now."

"I shall soon be fifteen," said Dorothy, drawing herself to her full height.

"Well, here's your chance to show what you're worth. If you can manage in this emergency, I shall have some opinion of you. I can telephone to the Nursing Institution if I find it's too much for you."

"I hope that won't be necessary," replied Dorothy.

In that one hour she seemed to have suddenly grown years older, and to have taken up a new burden of responsibility. Martha hardly knew her when she entered the sick room, she seemed so unwontedly calm and resourceful, yet withal so gentle, so tactful, and so deft and clever in doing all that was required for the invalid.

"I'd no idea the bairn could be so helpful," murmured Martha to herself. "If she goes on as well as she shapes, we'll do without a nurse, and that'll ease Miss Sherbourne's mind. She can't afford two guineas a week, let alone the woman's keep, and it would worry her to think of the expense. As far as I'm concerned I don't want a nurse in the house, making extra trouble and what waste goodness knows!"

The first thing Dorothy did when she could be spared from Aunt Barbara's room was to find her blotter and write a letter to Vera Norland. It ran thus:

> "Dear Vera,—Can you take the part of 'Queen of the Daffodils' instead of me? My aunt is very ill, and I am afraid I shall not be able to come to school for a while, so I shall miss the rehearsals. I thought I had better let you know at once, so that you will have time to get your dress.
>
> "Sincerely yours,
> "Dorothy Greenfield."

She ran out herself and posted the letter, then came back and quietly sat down again by Aunt Barbara's bedside. It cost her a great pang thus to give up her part in the festival, but once the irrevocable step was taken, and the letter in the pillar box, she felt much better.

"You've just got to forget about that pageant, Dorothy Greenfield," she said to herself. "You've been behaving abominably lately, and I'm thoroughly ashamed of you. Now's your chance indeed, as the doctor says. I only hope it hasn't come too late. Oh, you nasty, ungrateful, selfish, thoughtless thing, how I despise you!"

As Dr. Longton had anticipated, Miss Sherbourne had a sharp attack of her former complaint. For a week she lay very ill, and her two devoted nurses hardly left her day or night. It was a new experience to Dorothy to have Aunt Barbara, who had been accustomed to do everything for her, lying helpless and dependent upon her care. It brought out the grit in the girl's character, and made her see many things to which she had before been blind. Hitherto Dorothy had not been at all zealous at helping in the house, but now she cheerfully washed plates and dishes, and did many other tasks that were distasteful to her.

"'As one that serveth'" she often said to herself as she went about the daily duties, trying to take her fair share of the trouble and help poor, faithful Martha, whose devotion never slackened. She wore the little badge of the Guild constantly, that its remembrance might be always with her. "'As one that serveth'; Miss Tempest said that the motto ought to mean so much in one's life," she thought. "I didn't understand before, but I do now. When Auntie gets better, I'm going to be very different."

It was a joyful day for Martha and Dorothy when the doctor pronounced Miss Sherbourne out of danger.

"She has made a wonderful recovery," he said, "and if she only takes proper care of herself she ought to get on nicely now. She has had a splendid pair of nurses. Honestly, Dorothy, I never thought you would be able to manage without professional help. You've done very well, child, very well indeed."

This was high praise from bluff old Dr. Longton, and Dorothy flushed with pleasure. She was glad if she had been able, in the least degree, to return to Aunt Barbara any of the love and tenderness that the latter had lavished upon her for more than fourteen years. The debt was still so great, it seemed impossible ever to pay it back.

Once the fever had left her, Miss Sherbourne made rapid progress, and by the twelfth of May she was able to come downstairs for the first time.

Dorothy made the little dining-room so gay with flowers for her reception that it looked like a May Day festival.

"Why, sweetheart, this is the day of your school anniversary," said Aunt Barbara, as she and Dorothy sat at tea. "You ought to have been acting 'Queen of the Daffodils'."

"Don't talk of that, Auntie! I got Vera to take it instead."

Dorothy's eyes were full of tears.

"I'm sorry you were disappointed, darling."

"Auntie, it's not that; please don't misunderstand me. Ever since you were ill I've wanted to tell you that I know now what a nasty, ungrateful wretch I've been. You've been working and toiling for me all these years, and I took it just as a matter of course, and never thought how much you were giving up for me. I'm going to work for you now. I'm afraid I can't do much at first—with money, I mean—but I'll try my hardest at the Coll., and perhaps in a year or two I may be a help instead of a burden."

"A burden you have never been, child," said Miss Sherbourne. "If I had only got well a little sooner, we would have made you the costume. I sent the articles off the afternoon I was taken ill, and a cheque for them came a week ago."

"Then you must spend it on yourself, please. No, I'm glad the daffodil dress wasn't made. I should always have hated myself for having it."

"But you've missed the whole festival," regretted Aunt Barbara.

"Never mind, it's May Day here as well as at Avondale. Look at the lilac and the columbines, and this bowl of wallflowers! The air is so sweet and soft now, and there's a thrush's nest in the garden. All the harsh winds and the cold seem to be gone, and summer has come."

"Yes, summer has indeed come," said Aunt Barbara, gazing, not at the flowers, but at Dorothy's face, where a new, softened look had replaced the old frown of discontent.

CHAPTER XIV
WATER PLANTAIN

Dorothy returned to Avondale resolved to work doubly hard. There was certainly plenty to be done if she did not wish to fall behind in her Form. She had missed many of the lessons, and to recover the ground that she had lost meant studying the textbooks by herself, and trying to assimilate endless pages of arrears.

"Yet I must," she thought. "If I leave out the least scrap, that's sure to be the very piece I shall get in the exam. I'm going over every single line—though it's cruel translating Virgil and learning Racine in such big doses. Never mind, Dorothy Greenfield, you've got to do it. I shan't let you off, however much you hate it."

Faithful to her determination, Dorothy set the alarum in her bedroom for a quarter to six, and had nearly an hour and a half's study each morning before Martha called her at 7.15. It was very tempting sometimes to turn over and go to sleep again; but she soon began to grow quite used to her early rising, and it seemed almost a shame to stay in bed when the sun was up, and the thrush was singing cheerily in the elder bush outside.

A NURSING EXPERIENCE

The aim that Dorothy had in view was so ambitious that she hardly dared confess it even to herself. Every year a prize was given at Avondale called the William Scott Memorial. It was thus named after the founder of the College, who had left a sum of money in his will for the purpose. It was awarded annually to the girl in any form who obtained the highest percentage of marks in the examinations. Though it was generally gained by members of the Sixth, it did not of necessity fall to them; every girl had an equal opportunity, for it went entirely by their relative scores, the object being to distinguish the pupil who had worked the best, irrespective of age.

"I believe it fell once to the Second; but the Sixth have had it for four years now," thought Dorothy. "Time for a new departure. I don't suppose

I've the slightest ghost of a chance, but it's worth trying. I shan't mention my hopes to anybody, though—not even to Aunt Barbara—they're so remote."

Her increased efforts could not fail to win notice, however, at the College.

"Dorothy Greenfield, you're just swatting!" said Mavie Morris one day. "I don't believe you'd a fault in your last German exercise, and you recited all that Virgil without one single slip. What's come over you?"

"Nothing," replied Dorothy, turning a little red. "You talk as if I'd been committing a crime."

"So you have. You're raising the general average of the standard, and that's not fair to the rest of the Form. When Pittie sees you with three 'excellents' to your name, she thinks I ought to do the same."

"Why can't you?"

"Why? You ask me why? Do you think I'm going to muddle my brains more than I can help, just in the middle of the tennis season? You little know Mavie Morris. No, Dorothy, I've a distinct grievance against you. There you are now—actually surreptitiously squinting at a book while I'm talking to you!"

"It's not a lesson book, at any rate; it's from the library," retorted Dorothy.

"Let me look at it. You humbug, it's a Manual of Botany! I call that lessons, in all conscience."

"Well, it has jolly coloured illustrations," said Dorothy, trying to plead extenuating circumstances. "I want to hunt out the names of some specimens I've found. We have heaps of wild flowers growing in the lanes at Hurford."

"Whitewashed, but not exonerated! Your manual smacks too much of school for my taste. Why don't you take a leaf from me and practise tennis?"

"No luck for such a bad server as I am."

"Well, I didn't say you'd win the championship. I've no chance myself against Val and Margaret. Here's Alison; she'll reason with you. She isn't on the rising balance of the Form any more than I am myself. Alison, tell Dorothy to quit this everlasting studying. Don't you agree with me that it makes it far harder for us slackers?"

Alison laughed good-naturedly. She never troubled much about her own lessons, for her mother was generally so anxious regarding her health, and so afraid of her overworking herself, that an hour's preparation sufficed for her home work—and, indeed, if she took more, Mrs. Clarke would threaten to complain to Miss Tempest.

"Yes, Dorothy's turning into quite an old bookworm," she replied. "She even insisted on looking over her Latin in the train this morning. I can't stand that, because I always like to talk. I don't get too much of Dorothy's company."

It was still a grievance to Alison that her mother would not sanction any closer intimacy with her friend. She had hoped, after the visit to Ringborough, that matters would be on a different footing, and that she would be allowed to introduce Dorothy at home and invite her frequently. She could not understand why, for no apparently adequate reason, she must be debarred from her society. The fact that she was discouraged from being on too familiar terms had the effect of making her even more enthusiastic in her affection. There was a strong vein of obstinacy in her disposition, and if she once took up an idea she was apt to keep to it.

"Uncle David likes Dorothy," she argued. "He told Mother not to be ridiculous. I heard him say so. Perhaps in time I shall get my own way."

Mrs. Clarke, anxious not to thwart her darling more than was necessary, had many times proposed that some other classmate from Avondale should be asked to Lindenlea. But Alison had flatly refused.

"I can't possibly have Grace Russell or Ruth Harmon without inviting Dorothy. She'd think it most peculiar and unkind. No, Mother dearest, if I mayn't have her I'd rather not ask anybody at all."

"But you ought to have young companions, Birdie," protested Mrs. Clarke fretfully. "Your uncle was speaking to me on that very subject before he went to Scotland; and he is your guardian, so he is partly responsible for you. I believe I shall have to send you to a boarding school after all."

"No, no; I should be miserable, and so would you without me. I'd hate to leave the Coll. Don't worry, Motherkins, Uncle David shan't lecture you. Naughty fellow! I won't be friends with him if he hints at boarding school again."

"I shall certainly talk it over with him when he returns from Lochaber," said Mrs. Clarke.

"When is he coming back? Is he really going to take a house near here, Mother?"

"I don't know. He may possibly settle in the South, in which case I should certainly decide to remove, and to go and live near him."

"Oh, please no! I don't want to leave Latchworth or the Coll.," protested Alison.

Alison was indeed absolutely happy at Avondale. For a day school the arrangements were perfect, and there were many features of the course there which suited her tastes. She liked the Ambulance Guild and the Tennis Club, and both the gymnasium and the laboratory were large and specially well equipped, far more so than in most boarding schools. This term, also, Miss Carter, the science mistress, had begun a very interesting series of Nature Study lessons, which included birds and insects, and made a special point of botany; and Alison, who adored flowers, threw herself into it heart and soul. It was the one subject over which she really gave herself much trouble. She collected specimens and pressed them, identified them from the big volumes of "Sowerby" in the library at Lindenlea, mounted them on sheets of cardboard, and printed their names neatly underneath.

"I shall have something to send to the Arts and Crafts Exhibition," she said, "though I'm no good at anything else."

"No good! Fiddlesticks!" exclaimed Dorothy.

"True, my dear! Have you ever seen me top at an exam., or even second? Why, I only get 'excellent' once in a blue moon, and then I'm so astonished, I think it must be a mistake! I'm not picked out to play at school concerts, or recite, or act, or show off in any way. Oh, don't think I'm complaining! I don't crave for notoriety. There's nothing I detest worse than having to perform in public. But pressed flowers are different. I can do them in private at home, and let them be seen without exhibiting myself. I wish I could find a few more specimens. I believe I've picked everything that's to be had at Latchworth."

"Miss Carter promised she'd take us a botanizing ramble some afternoon," said Dorothy.

"So she did. We must keep her to her word. Let us try to catch her now in the corridor, and see if we can get her to name a definite day. Ask Mavie and Grace to come too. They're the keenest next to us."

The little group of enthusiasts waylaid the mistress as she came out of the library, and, reminding her of the projected expedition, nailed her to the point.

"Very well, we will decide on next Saturday afternoon, provided, of course, that it's a fine day," replied Miss Carter.

"And the place?" asked Alison.

"I think we can't do better than Beechfield. We could walk along the embankment to Longacre, and take the train back from there. We ought to find plenty of flowers on the way."

"And we might stop and have tea somewhere," suggested Alison, who was determined to make an outing of it.

"Yes, so we might. There's an inn by the river about half-way to Longacre, and several cottages that cater for visitors."

"We can start quite early, I suppose?"

"I'll look up the railway guide, and pin a programme on the notice board to-morrow."

"There, you see!" said Alison, as the deputation returned in triumph, "there's nothing like sticking to a thing. I believe in people keeping promises when they make them."

"We shall have a ripping afternoon. Miss Carter is ever so jolly."

"And I expect she'll be jollier still when she's 'off duty'."

Notwithstanding the tempting nature of the programme, only ten put down their names for the botanizing expedition. In summer there were many diversions for Saturday's holiday—the tennis season was in full swing, and the girls had attractions at their own homes that outweighed a country ramble.

"It's far nicer without too many," declared Alison. "I've been school excursions before, at Leamstead, and it's generally so hard to get everybody to come along. Half the party is always lagging behind, and then a dozen come running up and want all the explanations over again, just when the mistress has finished describing something. You waste an immense amount of time in collecting people. I mean to stick to Miss Carter like glue the whole afternoon."

"Absorbing information like a piece of blotting-paper!" laughed Mavie. "Quite a new character for you, Alison Clarke."

"Don't mock. You're as keen on going as I am myself."

The ten Nature students met Miss Carter at Coleminster station at half-past two on the Saturday, and started off for Beechfield, which was on a different line from Hurford and Latchworth. Neither Dorothy nor Alison knew the place, so to them at least it had the charm of novelty.

"I've often walked over the fields to Longacre," said Grace Russell, "but I don't mind going again. It will seem fresh if we're looking for flowers. I like an object when I'm out."

"And I like the fun of being out, object or no object," said Mavie. "I honestly confess I'm looking forward to tea-time."

"You shameless materialist!" said Miss Carter. "You shan't have a single cup unless you can name a dozen flowers. I shall put you through an examination first."

"I'll be attentive—with tea as my goal."

There was no doubt about it—Miss Carter was jolly. She talked and joked as merrily as the girls themselves, climbed stiles with agility, and, much to her pupils' amusement, exhibited an abject terror of cows.

"It was born in me, and I can't conquer it," she declared. "I suppose it's partly because I'm town-bred. The very sight of their horns puts me in a panic."

"I'll walk along first and shoo them away with my umbrella," said Dorothy, laughing.

"What heroism! I really envy your courage. To me the pleasures of botany are sadly spoilt by cows; there is invariably one in the meadow where I want to pick my best specimens."

In spite of her real or pretended fears, Miss Carter ventured to take the path which led over the fields to Longacre. It was a pretty walk, partly through a park shaded with beautiful trees, and partly along an embankment which formed the remains of an ancient fortification against the Danes. The hay was still uncut, so the fields were full of flowers, and without unduly trespassing into the long grass the girls were able to pick many specimens. Alison kept to her intention of sticking to Miss Carter, and scarcely left her side; she enjoyed the explanations, and passed them on to Mavie, who was collecting her dozen plants with ostentatious zeal. Dorothy was told off as policeman to bring up stragglers.

"We shall never get there at all if you can't keep together and come along," said Miss Carter. "I can see a little peep of the river, and one chimney of the inn over there in the distance. Don't you feel inclined for tea?"

"Rather!" agreed the girls, making a spurt.

The inn was one of those small, wayside places common in rural districts. It catered for anglers and tourists, and had a pretty, flowery garden, set with wooden benches and tables ready for picnic parties. It was a suitable spot for a halt; everyone felt warm with the walk, and disposed to welcome the sight of cups and saucers.

"How sweet it is here!" said Alison to Dorothy. "Something smells perfectly delicious—I don't know what."

"I think it must be honeysuckle down by the river."

"Then let us go and see. It's rather early for honeysuckle; I haven't found any out yet. It might perhaps be a sweetbrier. Tea isn't quite ready, so we shall have plenty of time."

The two girls strolled out of the garden and down a short lane that led to the river. It was beautiful there—the grassy banks were white with tall, lacy, umbelliferous plants, and groups of willows drooped their picturesque, shimmering boughs over the water.

"Look at the old weir," said Alison. "I believe there used to be a mill here once, only it isn't working now. Dorothy, what's that growing in the river? Isn't it water plantain?"

"It looks uncommonly like it."

"I must have a piece—I positively must! How can we get some? Do you think we could walk along the edge of the weir and reach it? It's only a few yards off."

"I dare say we might, if we could hold on to those willows."

"Let us try. Give me your hand."

"It's rather slippery," said Dorothy, as she essayed to follow.

Catching on to the branches of a willow, the two girls stepped cautiously along the uncovered stones at the edge of the weir towards the spot where the water plantain was growing so temptingly.

"There's a splendid piece almost within reach," said Alison. "Stick tight to my hand, Dorothy, and I'll bend over. I'm within an inch of it."

"Be careful!" exclaimed Dorothy. "Don't pull!"

But her warning came too late. Alison, in her effort to grasp the plantain, put her weight on her friend, and to support the strain Dorothy leaned backwards. Alison, snatching a piece of the flower, suddenly released the tension; the pair swayed for an instant, overbalanced, and then slipped, shrieking, down the sloping side of the weir.

CHAPTER XV
A CONFESSION

The two girls sank into the pool below, then, rising to the surface, caught with frantic fingers at a rotten willow bough that overhung the water. Neither could swim, and in desperate plight they clung to the frail and insecure support. Almost choked with their dipping, their hair and clothes streaming, they still managed to call vigorously for help. But already their weight was splitting the decayed old willow: there was an ominous crack, a sudden rending, a piteous cry, and, still clutching the severed branch, they went whirling down the river. Mercifully their first wild shriek had been heard, and a farmer who lived at the old millhouse by the weir had come running instantly from his garden. He arrived on the scene just as the branch broke, and wading into the water he contrived to catch Dorothy, who was the nearer, and to drag her into safety. But when he turned to look for her companion, Alison had drifted along with the stream, and was out of his reach. He could not swim, so he ran back towards the inn, shouting for help. At the sound of his cries the stable boy and several others came rushing down the field.

"Fetch a rope!"

"Where's the boat?"

"Cut a long pole!"

"She'll drown while you're doing it!"

"For Heaven's sake don't let her go down again!"

"I can only swim a few strokes, but I'll try if I can reach her," exclaimed the stable boy, flinging off his coat and plunging into the river, which was shallow for a yard or so at the edge.

Venturing out of his depth, he grasped Alison by her dress, then turned, floundering hopelessly towards the bank. For a moment it seemed as if both lives must surely be lost, but with a desperate effort the boy managed to keep himself afloat, and to reach the hand of one of the men who had waded out to meet him. Between them they pulled the unconscious girl from the water and laid her on the grass.

"She's gone!"

"No, no; I've seen worse than her as came round."

"Take 'em both into the inn and send Sam on his bike for the doctor."

The first intimation of the accident which Miss Carter received was the sight of Dorothy walking dripping wet up the garden, followed by a group of men carrying Alison. She was a woman of sound, practical common sense, and after the first momentary shock was over she set to work at once to administer treatment for the drowning, with the help of the other members of the Guild who were present. Their combined efforts were so successful that by the time the doctor arrived they had succeeded in restoring animation.

Dorothy, rolled up in hot blankets, was little the worse for her immersion, and did not need attention; but the medical man looked grave when he saw Alison.

"She is suffering from severe collapse. Have you sent for her mother?" he asked.

Miss Sherbourne and Mrs. Clarke had both been summoned by telegram. They drove up within five minutes of each other. Poor Mrs. Clarke's frantic, white-lipped agony was terrible to witness.

"You must save her! She's all I have in the world!" she cried, turning desperately, almost fiercely, upon the doctor.

"Madam, I use my utmost skill, but life and death are in greater hands than mine," he replied.

For many hours Alison's life trembled in the balance. The district nurse had been sent for, and with the doctor watched the case anxiously all night through. At length, when morning dawned, a turn came for the better.

"Let her sleep now and she'll do," said Dr. Hall to the nurse. "Can't we get her mother out of the room somehow?"

"Miss Sherbourne is downstairs. I know her, and I dare say she will help," suggested the nurse.

Aunt Barbara had also spent the night at the inn, partly because she thought it wiser to let Dorothy keep warm in bed, instead of attempting to remove her; and partly because she felt she could not leave till she knew that Alison was out of danger. She had sat up, hoping that she might be of assistance, though she had not liked to intrude her presence into the sick-room until she was asked. She came now at the nurse's request, and gently persuaded poor worn-out Mrs. Clarke to go downstairs and have some hot tea, which the inn-keeper's wife had made ready.

"It is better to leave the room in absolute quiet for a while," she said. "Nurse is keeping watch, and indeed the doctor says there is no further cause for anxiety."

Mrs. Clarke's hand shook as she held her cup.

"I can hardly realize yet that she is safe. Oh, if you knew how I have suffered! My head is on fire. I want to go out into the air," she replied pantingly.

The light was breaking clearly in the east, and Miss Sherbourne opened the front door. The two women stepped together into the garden.

"Everything seems quiet," said Mrs. Clarke, looking up at Alison's window. "You are sure, if there is the slightest change, that Nurse will call me? Then let us walk across the lawn. I want to talk to you. I must speak now—at once, while I have the courage."

"Shall we sit here?" said Miss Sherbourne, indicating a bench that faced the dawn.

The hour was strangely beautiful. The sky, flushing in tints of rose and mauve, heralded the rising sun; the bushes were still masses of rich, warm shadow, but a group of turn-cap lilies stood out fair and golden against the dark background, shedding their heavy fragrance around. A thrush had begun to stir in the laburnum tree, and piped his fine mellow notes; and a blackbird answered from the elm opposite. The world was waking to another day of wonderful, pulsing life.

"Weeping and heaviness may endure for a night, but joy cometh in the morning," murmured Aunt Barbara softly.

Mrs. Clarke sat for a few moments gazing at the quiet scene. She was still intensely agitated, and kept clasping and unclasping her hands nervously upon her knee.

"I must speak," she began again hurriedly. "If I do not tell you now, the resolution may go. When I saw my darling lie there, at the very gate of death, I knew it was a judgment upon me for my long silence—my criminal silence."

She paused, as if scarcely able to continue. She was weeping bitterly, and her restless fingers pulled to pieces a rose that she had plucked from a bush as she passed.

"I hardly know how to explain everything," she went on at last, "but perhaps it will make it clearer if I begin at the beginning, and relate the story of my life. Have you the patience to hear it? My sister Madeleine and I were twins. My mother died in our infancy, and left no other children, so we two were everything to each other. My father was a clever but eccentric man, a student and an astronomer. He had never been fond of company, and after my mother's death he shut himself up more closely than ever, and became quite a recluse, devoting himself entirely to his books and his telescope. Though he was fond of us in his way, we did not see much of him, and he was always so reserved and silent that we were shy and constrained in his presence. When we were old enough to leave school, our life at home, in a remote country grange, with little society to be had in the neighbourhood, was dull and triste in the extreme. Just after our twenty-first birthday, we made the acquaintance of two brothers who were staying at a house in the adjoining parish, and the friendship soon ripened into a warmer feeling on both sides.

"David Clarke, the elder, fell in love with my sister Madeleine, and Herbert, the younger, with myself. When we broached the subject to my father, however, he professed great indignation, and forbade either of the young Clarkes to come to the house. It was extremely arbitrary and unjust of him to behave thus, for he had no reasonable objections to raise against them. I can only imagine that he was annoyed that he had not been taken earlier into our confidence, and hurt that we wished to leave him. Perhaps, also, he may have had some other matrimonial projects in his mind for us, though he never made the slightest attempt to introduce us to any suitable friends. Can you imagine the situation? Two impulsive, motherless girls in the lonely old house, with no one to counsel us or help to smooth away any of our difficulties! Our lovers had business in India, and were shortly leaving the country; and the idea of parting from them was terrible to us. They pleaded and urged, so what wonder that there were clandestine meetings, and that one morning we took the law into our own hands and made a double runaway match of it? We were both of age, and could therefore legally marry whom we chose.

"We tried to make peace with our father after the weddings, but he utterly refused to see us, and we were obliged to start for India without having received his forgiveness. Within a year we had news of his death. I think he had been in failing health for some time, and perhaps on that account had been the more loath to part with us; but he had shown us so little tenderness that we had never realized that he wished for our sympathy or affection. Now that I have a child of my own, I regret that I was not a better daughter to him. In his will he showed that he had not pardoned either us or our husbands. He left only a small annuity each to Madeleine and myself, and the bulk of his estate in trust for his first grandchild. My sister Madeleine's little girl was born a fortnight before mine, so it was she, and not Alison, who inherited her grandfather's fortune. I was very angry at the injustice of the proceeding. It seemed to me monstrously unfair that my little one, because she came into the world a fortnight too late, should be deprived of what in all equity ought to have been hers. I was the elder of the twins, and I considered that any preference should have been in my favour. I was anxious to bring a lawsuit, and try to upset the will and cause the estate to be equally divided between my sister and myself, but our solicitor assured me I had no legal case, and should only involve myself in endless proceedings and costs. Madeleine and I were too much attached to each other to have an open quarrel, and before her I managed to hide my bitter disappointment. We were about to be separated, for my husband was returning to England, while hers was still remaining in India. I was thankful afterwards that we had parted on such good terms, for I never saw her again. Only a few days after our steamer started she succumbed to a sudden epidemic of cholera that swept over the place where they were living, and the telegram announcing her death met me at Port Said. I had loved her dearly, and the blow was cruel. But there was a harder one still in store for me. My husband, whose ill health had been the cause of our leaving India, became rapidly worse, and before I even realized the extent of the danger, he too was taken from me. In a single year I had lost father, sister, and husband, and at twenty-three I found myself a young widow, with an only child.

"At this juncture my brother-in-law, David Clarke, returned to England, bringing his motherless baby in charge of an ayah. He did not intend to stay, only to settle a few necessary business matters and to make some arrangement for his little girl, who was delicate, and could not be reared in India. He had no near relations of his own who were willing to be troubled with the child, so he asked me if I would undertake to bring her up with mine, and I accepted the charge. I was drawn to little Rosamond for her mother's sake, though I could never forgive her for being a fortnight older than her cousin. So everything was settled. I took a house in Scotland for the summer, which I thought would be healthy for the children, and I sent Alison on there in advance with her own nurse. The ayah who had brought Rosamond from India was to return in the same ship as my brother-in-law, who was starting immediately for Madras. He wanted to see his baby till the very last, so I accompanied him to London, taking with me Mrs. Burke, a respectable woman who had once been a maid at my father's house, and was now married, to act as temporary nurse after the ayah's departure.

"When the last good-byes were said, and my brother-in-law and the ayah had started, I found I wished to do some shopping in London before I went north. It is awkward and inconvenient to keep a baby at a hotel, so I determined to send Mrs. Burke with my little niece to Scotland, where my own responsible nurse was already settled in charge of Alison. I took them to the station and saw them safely off in the express. In a few days I intended to follow them. That very night, as I sat at dinner in the hotel, I heard the newsboys shouting 'Special edition', and learnt of a terrible northern railway smash. I set off by the first available train for the scene of the disaster. It was impossible to get beyond Burkden, for the line was disorganized, but I hired a carriage and went on to Greenfield. The first point to be ascertained was whether my niece was among the victims. I wasted some time enquiring at the railway offices, and it was not till late in the afternoon that I saw a newspaper poster with the heading: 'Baby's Wonderful Escape from the Accident'. It was only after further investigations and delays that I learnt the child was being taken care of by its rescuer at the Red Lion Hotel. Do you remember how I came into the inn parlour that evening? The scene is stamped vividly upon my memory. You sat by the fireside with the baby on your knee; the light falling from the hanging lamp above made a picture of you both. It had taken a fancy to you, though it was always shy with me, and its soft little cheek was pressed against your face. I looked at it, and I think if it had given one sign of recognition, or held out its arms to me, I should have claimed it. But it took no notice at all, and my heart hardened against it. A terrible temptation assailed me. If I disowned the baby, nobody would ever know its identity. It would be so easy to tell its father that it had perished in the fire; there could be no positive evidence about any of the victims of the disaster. If it were out of the way, then my baby would inherit the fortune which I had always considered was my due. I was not left well off, and money meant so much to me. I had not been brought up to study economy, and I hated to be poor. I am a good judge of character, and I knew from your face that you would not abandon the child you had saved.

I thought Fate had interfered forcibly, and had given it into your keeping instead of mine. At the moment it seemed to me a direct interposition of Providence, and a sign that my father's inheritance was not intended to be lost to me after all. Before me stood a great choice—the good of my sister's little one, or my own—and I chose my own. The sequel proved easy—only too easy. I said the baby I had seen at the inn was not my niece, and nobody doubted my word. My brother-in-law and the ayah were already on their way to India, Mrs. Burke was dead, and no one else was likely to raise the question of identity. The portrait circulated in the newspapers was such a poor snapshot that neither my nurse nor any of Mr. Clarke's relations recognized it. They had not known the child intimately; they had only seen her once or twice in her ayah's arms. Before I left the Red Lion at Greenfield I ascertained your name—I scarcely knew why; it seemed an instinct at the moment. I wished to forget it, but it remained all the same—one of those things which it is impossible to wine from one's remembrance.

"Years went by, years of prosperity, for in trust for Alison I was a rich woman. I tried to banish all thoughts of Rosamond, and to justify my action to myself, yet in my inmost heart I knew I had sinned. For some time I lived in the Midlands, but Leamstead did not suit my little girl's health, so I removed to Latchworth. When Alison started to go to the College and I first saw Dorothy in the train, I was immediately struck with her appearance. I could not think of whom she reminded me; her eyes haunted me continually. One day I came home and found that she had been at our house in my absence, and that Alison was full of her resemblance to the portrait of my sister Madeleine which hung in the drawing room. Then I knew, even without the extra links that made the connection only too plain—the story of her adoption, which Alison had heard at school; the very name of Dorothy Greenfield, and your name, which I had not succeeded in forgetting. Alarmed at the recognition, I forbade Alison to invite her again, and in every way in my power discouraged the acquaintance between the two girls. I thought of removing from Latchworth, but I had taken my house on a lease and spent much on improving it. Everything appeared to conspire against me: first Alison's extreme affection for Dorothy, then our meeting at the Hydro., where my brother-in-law, unaware of her identity, was so charmed with his daughter. Then came Alison's visit to your cottage on the afternoon when I fetched her in the pony trap. I at once recognized your servant as the one I had seen in the inn parlour at Greenfield, and I could tell by her face that she remembered me. It seemed as if Fate, whom I thought I had conquered so successfully, was dogging my footsteps. I felt my position was most unsafe, and only yesterday afternoon I definitely decided to sacrifice the improvements I had made at Lindenlea and to remove to the south of England, where there would be no further chance of Dorothy crossing our path.

"As if in direct consequence of my determination followed this terrible accident. It seemed to me like Heaven's vengeance on my sin. Was my innocent child to suffer as the scapegoat for my wrongdoing? I vowed to God that if in His mercy He would spare her life, I would make a full confession and reparation, no matter what it cost me. There, I have told you the whole. Do you despise me utterly? Can you possibly ever forgive me that I deliberately thrust the child upon you, and let you bear so heavy a burden all this time? Her own father will be only too thankful to take her now."

Miss Sherbourne's face was turned towards the golden streak of dawn. For a few moments she was silent.

"We have both so much to be thankful for this morning, that it makes it easier to forgive," she said at last. "Yes, the wrong must be righted, and father and daughter restored to each other; but I am glad I was able to keep my little Dorothy for my own those fourteen happy years."

CHAPTER XVI
THE WILLIAM SCOTT PRIZE

Dorothy, who was little the worse for her dangerous experience, went home on the morning following the accident, but it was several days before Alison was able to be removed from the inn. She was not a strong girl, and the fright and immersion combined had produced a state of complete exhaustion. The quiet and rest which the doctor prescribed had, however, their due effect, and by the end of a week she began to seem her old self again. The surprise of the two girls when later they learnt the news of their relationship can be imagined. Mrs. Clarke wrote to her brother-in-law, making a full avowal of everything; and though at first he found it hard to grant her the forgiveness she implored, his delight at finding his daughter alive outweighed his anger at the long and cruel course of deception that had been practised upon him. For the sake of Alison, to whom he was much attached, he allowed himself to be reconciled to his sister-in-law, and agreed to forget the past and let bygones be bygones. Both he and Miss Sherbourne decided emphatically that Mrs. Clarke's share in the story must be kept a strict secret among themselves; it was most undesirable that either Dorothy or Alison should know of the dishonourable part she had played. To both the girls and the outside public it was enough to announce, without detailed explanations, that the mystery of Dorothy's parentage had been solved. Martha, the only other person who had guessed at the facts of the situation, could be safely trusted to preserve silence.

"I shall not at present claim for my daughter the fortune which is legally hers," said Mr. Clarke. "I do not need it, for I have been very successful financially in India, and am now in comfortable circumstances and able to retire from business. I could not see my brother's child in poverty, so the trust money must still be devoted to Alison's benefit. When Rosamond is twenty-one, and of age to decide such matters for herself, I hope that she will agree to divide the legacy equally with her cousin, and thus set right what was originally a most unjust will."

To Dorothy the discovery was both a delight and a pain. It removed the stigma that she considered had formerly attached to her, and placed her in the position of other girls as regarded name and family; but it had certain drawbacks which must be faced. Though she welcomed her newly-found father, she clung passionately to the one friend who had hitherto made the sum of her life.

"Aunt Barbara has brought me up and done everything for me. I can't leave her. I've promised to work for her and take care of her when I am old enough," she said earnestly.

"I know, child. I know what we owe her. You and I will look after Aunt Barbara together," replied Mr. Clarke.

Dorothy's news made a great sensation at the College. The romantic story appealed to the girls, and congratulations poured in upon her. Even Hope Lawson and Valentine Barnett waxed cordial.

"We've never had such an excitement at school before," declared Ruth Harmon. "It's the most interesting thing I've ever come across in my life."

"We don't know what to call you now," laughed Mavie Morris. "You're Dorothy Greenfield, alias Rosamond Clarke. Which is it to be?"

"Dorothy Greenfield, please, till the end of the term. Next session my new name can be entered on the College register, and I'll start in a fresh character."

"Then in the meantime we'll call you Rosador, as a compromise."

There was very little of the term left now, for the examinations were to begin the next week, and after those were over would come the annual speech day, which always concluded the school year. Dorothy's studies had naturally been somewhat upset by the recent course of events, but she had made an extra spurt at her work, and did not feel herself ill prepared. She rather liked examinations. She had a clear head and a good memory, and a neat, concise method of setting forth her information.

"I think it's quite inspiring to see a pile of fresh sheets of foolscap and a paper of questions," she declared.

"Yes, if you can answer the questions," returned Mavie. "It's a different matter if one's stumped. I'm utterly against the competitive system."

Dorothy laughed.

"State your reasons, Mavie," urged Ruth Harmon. "We'll set 'The Competitive System' as a subject for the Debating Society."

"Well, to begin with, emulation is the wrong spirit in which to promote work."

"A grand sentiment—but nothing would promote work in you, you dear old lazybones, so it's no use arguing the point."

"Very well. If I'm content to absorb my knowledge in homeopathic doses, why must I be worried into swallowing more than I can digest? If I were running a school I'd allow the clever girls who wanted to go in for exams, to take them, and let the others alone. I call it sheer cruelty to put the ordinary rank and file on the rack. Next week will be purgatory to me. You'll see me pining day by day, and gradually wasting away."

In spite of Mavie's forebodings, she survived the ordeal of the examination, and presented her usual appearance of robust health at the end of the dreaded period.

"I've done badly, though," she protested. "I expect I've failed in at least half my subjects. The maths. was detestable and the geometry simply wicked. Rosador, you're looking very smug. I believe you liked the papers."

"They weren't bad, as papers go," returned Dorothy. She did not care to boast, but she was conscious that she had done well, and reached a mark far above her average standard.

"Still, one never knows," she thought. "Exams. are uncertain things, and heaps of other girls may have done better than I have. I just won't think about the results."

Governors' Day, as it was popularly called, was always rather a grand occasion at Avondale. The school was a famous one in the town, and numbered among its pupils many who came from the best families in Coleminster. The governors liked to assure the parents that the College was keeping up its well-earned reputation for efficiency, and to give some opportunity for a general exhibition of the work done during the year. With this end in view, the programme was representative of all branches of the curriculum. A show of drawings, paintings, and handicrafts done by the art classes was on view in the studio; the collections of pressed flowers and natural objects made in connection with the Nature Study Union were put up round the walls of the museum; and the Charity Basket garments contributed by the Ambulance Guild were spread out in the Juniors' Common Room. There were to be recitations in French and German, songs and instrumental music, speeches by the governors, and the head mistress's report on the examination results and the general progress of the whole school.

"I like the dear old Coll. when it's turned upside down like this," said Ruth Harmon, who, with Dorothy, had been told off as a steward for the occasion. "What a fearful cram! The people are simply pouring in. I don't know how we're to find seats for everybody."

"It is amazing how many the room will hold," said Dorothy. "They're bringing in more chairs, and people will have to sit very close together on the benches."

Dorothy was looking charming that afternoon, with an unwonted colour in her cheeks, and her fluffy brown hair tied back with a blue ribbon that matched the tasteful dress her father had provided for her. All the old angularity had slipped away from her lately, and a new graciousness and sweetness had taken its place.

"Dorothy Greenfield is like a hard, tight bud that has suddenly opened into a flower," commented Miss Carter, who was quick to notice the improvement.

The lecture hall was filling rapidly with guests, and the stewards had to be indefatigable in their exertions.

"I want to be here, there, and everywhere at once," said Ruth. "I wish I were a conjurer, and could contrive two chairs out of one. Someone is smiling at you near the door, Dorothy."

It was Percy Helm, who, with his father and mother and Eric, was making his way through the crush. Dorothy went to meet them and find them places.

"Gabrielle is on the platform with the chorus, and Norma is among her own Form," she whispered.

"And where are you going to sit?" asked Percy.

"Oh, I'm a wandering Jew at present. I shall slip in somewhere at the last."

Promptly at three o'clock the proceedings began, and Dorothy, her duties over for the present, found a corner that had been reserved for her on the platform. From her seat she had a very good view of the hall. How pretty it looked, she thought, with its decorations of flags and flowers, and its throng of interested faces! In the fifth row, not very far away, she could see her father with Mrs. Clarke, and dear Aunt Barbara. Dr. and Mrs. Longton were also present, and the Vicar of Hurford and his wife. The Helms were beaming at her from the back row.

"All my best friends are here to-day," said Dorothy to herself.

The first part of the programme was musical; glees were sung by picked members of the singing classes, and a few solos, both vocal and instrumental, were given. Alison, who had been taking violin lessons, played in a quartette and acquitted herself very creditably, in spite of a sudden panic of bashfulness. She came and sat beside Dorothy as soon as her part was finished.

"I'm so thankful it's over," she whispered. "I do so hate doing anything in public. I could see Mother looking at me all the time; I believe she was as nervous as myself. My hand shook so dreadfully at first, I could hardly hold my bow."

"Never mind, it sounded quite right," replied Dorothy. "Everybody applauded, especially Father."

"Yes, I saw Uncle David clapping hard. When are the exam. lists to be read? Have you heard?"

"Not until after the interval, so Miss Pitman says. They're to come with the speeches."

The recitations passed off well, Grace Russell, the only member of the Upper Fourth who took part in them, distinguishing herself particularly.

"Grace is A1 at languages," commented Alison. "She gets that tripping French accent most beautifully."

At four o'clock there was an interval, and the audience adjourned for tea and to see the exhibits. Alison's collection of pressed flowers was among those on view in the museum, and she bore off her particular circle of friends to look at it.

"It's got 'Highly Commended'," she remarked gleefully. "Uncle David, that's the very piece of rock rose you climbed up the cliff to pick for me—don't you remember it? Miss Sherbourne, you sent me that catchfly from Hurford. I got most of my flowers at Latchworth, and just a few from Beechfield. Do you recognize this? It's the water plantain. The innkeeper at Longacre brought me a big bunch of it just before I left. Wasn't it kind of him? I keep it as a specimen, and as a memento of my dipping as well."

Alison spoke brightly. She had not been told how serious her collapse had been after her rescue from the river; and she little knew what an important share the water plantain had played in bringing about the happy reunion between her uncle and cousin.

"Dorothy has 'Commended' for her drawing from the cast," she continued, dragging Uncle David to the other side of the room. "Isn't it good? It's the head of Clytie up there, so you can see how like it is. And we've both got 'Neatly Rendered' for our Guild garments. Yes, yes, Uncle; you must come and see them, even if you don't know anything about sewing. Mine's the flannel jacket, and Dorothy's is the child's nightdress. We did every stitch of them ourselves."

"Did you bake the cake that has just disagreed with me at tea?" enquired Mr. Clarke, with a twinkle in his eye.

"No, you naughty man! We don't have cookery classes. When we do, I'll take care to bring something home, and insist upon your eating it, every crumb. Now, we've shown you all our exhibits, and we must go downstairs again and take our places. The speechifying is going to begin directly."

The second part of the programme represented the real business of the afternoon. Alderman Herbert, the chairman of the committee of the College, gave an opening address upon the general aims and objects of the system of education pursued at the school; and this was followed by Miss Tempest's report on the work done during the year. Then came the examination lists. Dorothy listened eagerly. She had done well, certainly; but until the final scores were read, it was impossible to compare her results with those of the top girls in other Forms. She was the best in the Upper Fourth, but probably one of the divisions of the Sixth might be able to produce an even higher record.

At the end of the lists Miss Tempest paused.

"Before continuing," she said, "I should like to give a word of explanation as to the terms upon which the William Scott Memorial is awarded. It is a prize which was bequeathed by the founder of the College to be given annually to whichever girl has gained the highest percentage of marks in the examinations. This year the honour falls to the Upper Fourth Form, where Dorothy Greenfield has gained 987 out of a possible 1000."

Dorothy listened like one in a dream. She could scarcely believe the evidence of her own ears. But it was true, for Alison was nudging her, and the other girls were whispering to her to "go forward". Very shyly she rose and walked to the front of the platform, where Alderman Herbert was beckoning her.

"I think we may all congratulate the lucky winner of the William Scott Memorial," he said, laying a kindly hand on Dorothy's shoulder. "Such success can only be the result of hard work and sustained effort. The Upper Fourth may well be proud of its record. I have much pleasure, my dear, in presenting you with this watch, which has been chosen for the prize."

As he spoke, he handed Dorothy a morocco case, and taking the beautiful little blue-enamelled watch from its satin bed, he pinned it on to her dress. The audience broke into a storm of applause. Dorothy had grown popular lately among the girls, and many of their parents had heard of the strange circumstances of her loss and finding. She received quite an ovation as she stood, smiling and blushing, by the side of the chairman.

"I'm so delighted," exclaimed Alison, as Dorothy returned to her place. "Let me look. Oh, what a ducky little watch! It's the prettiest I've ever seen.

But it isn't *that* I care about so much—it's the honour of winning. To think that our Form has got the Memorial! You dear, clever, industrious busy bee! I can't tell you how proud I am you're my relation."

"I'm glad my last appearance as Dorothy Greenfield has been a favourable one," laughed Dorothy. "Next term I shall be on the school register as Rosamond Clarke."

And here we must take leave of the cousins, for their story is all told. Mr. Clarke has bought a charming house at Latchworth, and is very busy furnishing it so that it may be ready for a certain occasion to which he is looking forward greatly. He is tired of Indian life, and has decided to settle down permanently in England. Dorothy is keenly interested in her new home, and especially pleased that it is so near to Lindenlea, and that she and Alison can still travel by train together to the College. As for Aunt Barbara, before the summer is over Dorothy will have learnt to call her by a dearer name still, and Holly Cottage will be to let.

www.ingramcontent.com/pod-product-compliance
Lightning Source LLC
LaVergne TN
LVHW052241280125
802434LV00032B/532